THE McCADE DRAGON BOOK 2

KATHI S. BARTON

World Castle Publishing, LLC
Pensacola, Florida
Copyright © Kathi S. Barton 2016
Hardback ISBN: 9781629895123
Paperback ISBN: 9781629895130
eBook ISBN: 9781629895147
First Edition World Castle Publishing, LLC, August 8, 2016
http://www.worldcastlepublishing.com

Licensing Notes

Cover: Karen Fuller
Editor: Maxine Bringenberg

CHAPTER 1

Jasmine Tyler moved along the boxes, her heart not into looking for a deal. She was exhausted, her body hurt in more places than she could think about, and she was lonely. With all the people around her she knew that was silly, but she missed her son and her grannie. It had been necessary to send them ahead. Ahead to what she wasn't entirely sure, but they were safer there than they were with her at the moment.

While I cannot see them as yet, I know they will be safe. Jasmine told the dragon that they'd better be. *I wish that you could talk to them. At least young Gavin. I think it would do you well to hear his voice. Him as well, I would bet. The boy loves you very much.*

And I love him very much as well. But you know as well as I that I can't chance contacting either of them. He said that he knew, but it made it no less sad for him too. *I'll be there soon, and when I am, I can get these earrings to the right person, gather him and Grannie up, and move on. And if you tell me again that I can't do that, then I swear to you that I'll cut my own ears off and be done with the lot of you.*

So the dragon didn't bother telling her again that it didn't work that way. Twice now she'd told him that if he brought up again how this man and his family would keep her and her family safe, she would never speak to him again. And the three days that she didn't say a single word had made her point for a little while. The dragon, or whatever manifestation he was to her, didn't listen well, it seemed.

She was going to have to move again soon. Making her way to this family was costing her so much more than just being without her family. Jasmine could hardly do any business with the way things were going, and it was more than a little difficult to trust anyone enough to even see if they were really a buyer for her things or someone out to get her. She shivered when she thought of what had happened to her and Gavin to get her moving out of their home in the first place.

They'd been headed to the post office, her and him, and they were going to get some pizza to take back to the house with them to share with her grannie. Gavin was telling her what homework he'd done that day and she was teasing him about working on the weekend. The car that hit them in the rear had come out of nowhere.

Being rear-ended really hadn't been that bad. Her truck was old and made before plastic was a big deal, and thankfully had no airbags or they might not have been able to get moving so quickly. For the most part they'd been all right, thankfully. But before she could get out of her truck to see what damage, if any, had been done to her truck, the man hit her again, then again. It was then that she realized he was pushing her into oncoming traffic. Screaming at Gavin to lay down on the floor, she floored the gas pedal and closed her eyes.

Still to this day she had no idea how she had managed to

not only get through the traffic, which had been very heavy and fast, but also escape whoever had tried to kill them. But as soon as she got home, she realized two things at once.

First, the dragon had been right. They were upset about the earrings and were coming for her. And the worst part of it was, they were also going to harm her son and grandmother. Secondly, they had to get out now. Not just out of the house, but they had to leave almost everything behind and get the fuck out of dodge.

Less than two hours after they got home, her truck was loaded and coolers packed, then they were gone. Even as they were driving through her little town, she saw three large black SUVs pass her going in the opposite direction from the one she was driving…the way toward her home. There were no plates on the big vehicles, and since the windows were so dark, she had no idea who or how many people were in them. Probably a good thing, she realized later.

She tried to tell herself that they might have been headed in any direction other than her house. But two days after they left the only home they'd had, she'd seen on the news that it had been burned to the ground, as had the barn that stood next to it. Jasmine gathered them up once again and made another long trip before she felt she needed information from the dragon in her head.

What is it about these earrings that has men trying to kill me for them? And why can't I take them out now that they're in my ears? I don't want to hear about how I'm going to this family, I want to know why I have to. Why me?

I can do that, my lady. There are six parts to me, a set of jewelry called a demi parvure. *It simply means matching set of jewelry. Few know that it was forged by a dragon and his master. They decided, when things were too dangerous for a dragon to be roaming the earth, that it would be safer if he, this being a part of me as a dragon, should have his spark, his magic, put within a special piece of jewelry. But alas, the magic was too much for a single piece and was divided up into five pieces. The sixth was made later when a lady thought the necklace was too large for anyone to wear. Then a terrible tragedy was bestowed upon the master and the dragon, along with all of his estate being taken away. I know not what happened to his things; only that the spark that creates us was no longer together.* Jasmine asked him how long ago this was. *I have no way of knowing that, my lady. For as a spark and only a small part of the whole, I cannot understand the passing of time until I have been awakened. But the ring, it has been awakened and thus, myself as well. And now it is held in trust by Emma...I have told you about her. The rest, not including yours, was spread out all over the world at one time, but now are close, but since the other pieces haven't been awakened yet, I know not where.* Her next question to him was, why her. *I know not, my lady. Until you touched the jewelry that has turned out to be my wings, I knew nothing of the holder.*

So, you want me to believe that there is this set of jewelry out there that a bunch of women will touch and bring to life...or I guess, bring you to life. Then if that doesn't sound creepy enough, these women have to make their way to this family of men, dragon men, and give it over to them and become their slave of sorts. And on top of that, they're stuck with this stuff forever, even if they want no part of this plot. I'm sorry, but this is about as farfetched as it gets. Not to mention sort of like slave trade for me to believe in. He asked her how she was hearing him if he was just a manifestation. *I don't know. A tumor? Could be. I've been under a lot of stress lately.*

You have, and I'm sorry to say that it isn't over as yet. When those men went to your home and destroyed everything that you had, they did a search and found enough information to find you and your family. She asked him what sort of information. *Pictures of you and your family. What Emma says is DNA on objects left behind. They can and will use every item in their possession to find you.*

And then what? What is it they think they're going to do to me? He didn't answer her. *Is my son in danger? My grannie?*

Yes. You all are until you can get to the McCade family. And even then, they will not stop until they either get what they desire or they are caught by the authorities. I am sorry, my lady. She wanted to cry. All she'd done was find a pretty pair of earrings that she wished she'd never seen now. *It would not have mattered when you saw them, my lady; somehow they would have come to you. You are the one that needs to be a part of the dragon with one of the McCade men.*

I don't want to be a part of any man. Don't you see? I've lost enough shit in my life because of a man. Not all of it was his fault, but he lied to me. Over and over, and there is no reason to think that this man won't too. He'll take and take until I have nothing. I am nothing. The dragon wisely said nothing. *I know; I'll mail them to them.*

You cannot remove them now that you wear them. Stomping her foot, she paced in front of the pretty little hotel where she'd stopped to rest for the night. *These terrible men, they will not stop until they have what they want. You must understand this.*

No, I don't have to understand anything. She turned when she heard Gavin call out to her. "I'm sorry, baby. What is it? Everything all right?"

"Yes. Why are you talking to yourself? Or it is that dragon again? Tell him that we're doing the best we can and to cut you some slack." She hugged him to her and felt tears fill her eyes. "We're going to be all right, aren't we, Mom? As soon as we get to this house, we're going to be just fine, right?"

"I hope so, Gavin, I really do."

Then five days after that, nearly two weeks ago now, she'd used every penny she had and put them both, her grandma and son, on a plane for Ohio. It wasn't safe for them to travel together any longer.

She was just sorting through a box when she felt something, a kind of nervous panic, which had her snatching her hand back from the items in the box and looking around. Christ, would she ever feel safe again, she asked herself? Then the dragon spoke to her, his voice calm yet slightly tight sounding.

The man near the food truck. Do you see him? Jasmine looked around, trying her best to look as if she were checking out the rest of the items. *He feels wrong.*

As casually as she could, Jasmine made her way to where she could get a better look at the man. She could see him now; he stood out like a man in a tux among a room of cowboys. At the moment he was trying to figure out how to eat a hotdog without wearing most of it. Backing into the trees and away from the man, she watched him unobserved for several minutes. There wasn't anything odd about him, nothing that she could say, "Hey, that's it," but she still knew there was something. She nearly told the dragon that he was looking for things that weren't there when the man shifted on his feet and she saw the gun.

The need to flee made her feel like she was being watched. Looking around, trying to decide what to do now, she wanted to curl into a tight ball and just cry. She had no car, nothing to protect herself with, and not a great deal of money either. She was, in a word, fucked.

I can't leave yet. Can I?

The dragon told her that she could not. Then he pointed out the man across the table from the auctioneer. He wasn't watching the items but looking around, as if he were searching the people and not what to buy next. Jasmine went deeper into the woods and then stood behind a tree. When the two men came together, they scanned the area twice before splitting up and moving around. She knew they were looking for her.

What do I do now? He told her not to move, not to run. *I can't let them get to me. If they do, you said that they'd kill me for these earrings. And as much as I hate the earrings right now, I need to get to my son, damn it.*

Do not move, my lady. They are looking for a young boy to be with you. They are thinking that you'd not leave him or your grandmother alone while they are out there. They know not that you have sent them both ahead. She let out a long breath and tried to think about anything but wanting to run. *If you do, then all is lost. Just wait for me to tell you that you can go. But to the bus stop, not to the hotel.*

She knew as surely as she was standing there listening to a dragon talk to her in her head that they'd already been to her hotel room and had figured out where she was. The newspaper. She'd gotten one and had circled the auction for today not far from where she'd been staying. It wasn't as if she had any money to spend—she didn't—but Jasmine was bored and needed to do something that didn't involve her thinking about how much she missed her son. So walking to the place that was stated in the ad, she had been there for only a few minutes when she realized it wasn't as fun as it used to be.

He is going to go by you in a few moments, and when he does, follow him, but not closely. I will tell you when to move to the bus stop. She wanted to tell him to fuck off, there wasn't any way she was going to follow that man, but the dragon spoke again before she could. *He will not expect you to be behind him. Nor will his partner. You must trust me on this. I will not allow you to be harmed.*

11

As soon as she was given the signal to move, Jasmine moved out from behind the tree and right behind the man. She was close enough that she could see the tat on the back of his neck that looked like some sort of Japanese symbol; or Chinese, she wasn't sure. There was also one that peeked out of the bottom of his sleeve. When he pulled the shirt up enough, she nearly stopped walking. Dragon told her to keep moving.

I've seen that before. He told her to turn then, and to go to the bus stop. When she did, the bus pulled up just as the man turned to go back to where she'd been. Sitting down, she turned on her seat and watched as both men moved around the yard again. *He had a dragon tat on his arm. I've seen that before. The man that tried to shoot us the day that Gavin got hurt and I sent them away. He had one just like it.*

They are all a part of a group of men out to harm you and all that help you. They have no wish to bring me to life, but to profit from controlling me. It is them that I am trying to save you from. Jasmine asked the dragon who they were, and what the writing meant. *It's Chinese, as you have guessed. It says* Sǐwáng de suǒyǒu lóng. *Its translation is, death to all dragons. I have not seen that for many years. More than you can imagine. It, like a great many things, comes and goes as the need arises. Today they need it to feel important. Who knows what it will be used for in the future.*

Her mind went in a single straight line direction. A group of men. Not a man, but a group. And they didn't just want her dead for the earrings, but they wanted to control the dragon himself. That meant that the McCades, the very people that she was headed to, were in danger as well. And her son and grannie would be caught up in it because she had blindly sent them there. Christ, she wanted to crawl into a hole and cry. To just bawl her eyes out. But now she had to make her way to Ohio faster, to see to her family. And the only way to do that was go get some money to get herself a car. She told the dragon what she needed and why.

I will help you. She nodded. He'd suggested that before, him helping her, but she'd told him that she would never cheat, steal, or lie to get what she needed. She'd had that done to her more than enough. *You will see; I'll keep you as safe as I can.*

And my family? How will you protect them? He told her that until they connected with the McCades he had no way of knowing about her son and grandmother. *And they won't until I get there. This is really fucked up; you know that, don't you?*

He said nothing, which was good...she wasn't ready for him to tell her anything but that they were going to make it. How, she hadn't any idea, but she so wanted to hear him say that to her. And as surely as she was sitting there, she knew that there was a lot more shit to deal with before she got to her son.

~~~

Jorden put the last of his paints in the box and set it on the floor. When he looked up, his entire being froze. The kid, a little boy, was standing there so still that he looked like one of his plaster casts. Jorden started forward to find out what he wanted when the kid lifted a gun and pointed it, steadily no less, right at him. Jorden stopped.

"I'm not going to hurt you." The kid said nothing. There were lines of exhaustion under his eyes, and his face looked puffy, as if he'd been crying recently. "If you're here to get some money or drugs, I'm afraid that I'm not going to be able to help you. I have neither here. The doctor isn't in either."

"It says there is a doctor here. There's a name downstairs on the door. It's the only reason I'm here. To get a doctor to

13

come with me. It says McCade. Where is he?" Jorden tried to think where Kenton was when the little boy spoke again. "It doesn't smell like a doctor's office up here either. More like Mrs. Witt's art class. Is he a physician or some other sort of doctor?"

"No, he's a physician. A general practitioner, as a matter of fact. And this is where I work, the reason for the smell. I'm an artist. Well, people tell me I am, and that I'm pretty good at it, I guess." He took a step forward and the kid told him to stop. "Do you need a doctor? I can call him here if you need him. Kenton, he's the doctor, he's off today with his wife doing.... Actually, I have no idea where he is. But if he's not here, then he's at his home."

"I don't know what else to do. I've been...I got up and she wouldn't wake up. So I thought that I could find a doctor. But I know that she's not going to be all right. My grannie, I believe she's died." Jorden nodded and sat down on the floor. He wanted to give the kid the impression that he was relaxed when he was anything but. "I need someone to come and look to make sure that I didn't do something wrong. We're on the run, my grannie and I."

"What might you have done to her?" He just shrugged. Jorden decided to ignore the part where they were on the run for now. "I see. So you think you killed her then?"

"No. I didn't kill her. She and I have been.... Last night she told me she was tired. She has been a lot lately. Powerfully tired she told me, and wanted to turn in early. So I was really quiet and got my shower and jammies on and played on my reader before I went to bed as well. When she didn't get up before I did, I checked on her and her face and neck were cold. I think she might have died in her sleep last night or sometime." The little boy scrubbed at his face and Jorden felt

14

badly for him. "I can't get in touch with my mom either. I'm all alone, so I thought a doctor could tell me for sure."

"Where is she...your grannie, I mean?" The kid said nothing but did lower the gun. "I'm going to get my cell phone out and call Kenton. And when he gets here, we'll go to where she is and we'll call in the police to—" The gun came up again, this time a little less steady. For some reason that scared Jorden more than the steady handling of the gun had.

"No, you can't do that. If you call the police, I'm as good as dead as I think she is." Jorden felt his dragon move along his skin. Fear and sadness made him want to go to the young kid and hold him. "Mom, she sent us ahead of her so that we'd be safe. And we've been doing everything we was told. But Grannie was sick before. It was why we went to stay with her."

Jorden pulled out his phone and pressed the button to call his brother. The kid never moved, just stood there with the 9mm pointed at him like he would most assuredly use it if he fucked up. When Kenton answered his cell laughing, Jorden almost wanted to hang up and call someone that wasn't having as good a day as Kenton seemed to be having.

"Did you decide that you needed some help moving out anyway? I told you that it was—"

Jorden cut his brother off. "I've got a visitor."

Kenton must have noticed something in his voice and asked him through their link who it was. "I have to speak to you this way. He has a gun pointed at me, and I don't want to be shot if it's all the same to you."

"I'm on my way." Jorden told him to just come alone. No police. "I'm not going to fucking come into a situation without some sort of back-up. You want me to tell Mom that you got us both hurt? You know how well that might go over."

"Kenton, you're going to have to trust me on this and

come here alone. I'm talking to him now. I would say that he's about ten or so years old." The kid told him how old he was. "He's ten. Just last week as a matter of fact. He came here looking for a doctor. A doctor named McCade. He said his grandma didn't wake this morning. And that he has been sent here ahead of his mom so that they'd be safe. He said that he's all alone in this world."

Kenton put together a string of curse words that made him smile. "Dragon said to ask him if he is Gavin. If his mom is Jasmine." Jorden asked and Gavin said that was right. "She's another part. The wings. Dragon said that she's fine, but he had no way of keeping in contact with the boy and his mom until one or both of them found us. I'm assuming that's why he doesn't want the police or the media involved. His mom is protecting him even now."

"Christ." Gavin lifted the gun again after having just put it at his side. Jorden had a feeling that he was making him nervous. "Come here first and bring Mom. I have no idea why, but I think he could use her. I know that I could right now."

"I'm on my way. I've contacted Dalton as well. He's not in uniform right now, so that might not be so bad. Can you ask Gavin if he is hurt?" Again he asked the boy, who just stared at him. "Jorden, did he tell you where his grandma is? Or where his mom might be?"

"No. He said that his mom sent them ahead and that his grandma didn't wake up." Jorden reached out to Kenton on their link. *I think he's hurting, but not physically. Also, he looks exhausted, and I can hear his belly growling from here. If he's been on the run since Dragon told you that she was coming, then they've been on the run for over a month.*

Poor kid. Christ, to try and stay safe like this and to have your grandmother die would be horrific. The kid has guts; I'll give him that. Jorden agreed, but told him he still had a gun pointed at him. *It'll be fine, Jorden. I'm at the door now. Can you warn him that I'm here?*

Jorden said that he would and the elevator motor kicked on, telling him that Kenton must have been right in the lift when he told him. Jorden watched as Gavin lifted the gun again and pointed it at him. It wasn't nearly as steady, and when he lowered it once again, Jorden realized how heavy it must have been for this kid.

"My brother. He's coming up with my mom." Gavin said nothing, but swayed just a little. "We won't hurt you, Gavin. We will protect you."

"The dragon, he told my mom that she needed to go to the McCade family and give them the earrings. He said that we'd be safe here. I'm not saying you had anything to do with my grannie dying, but I don't really feel very safe right now." Jorden nodded and watched his brother and mom come out of the elevator as Gavin continued. "He warned us the night that these men showed up at the hotel we were in. I was going to the bathroom when the door just flew open and there they were. One of them cut me with a knife when Mom said she couldn't give him whatever jewelry that she'd stolen from them. My mom doesn't steal. But they weren't taking no for an answer. So she hit the big one with a bat, then she shot the second guy. We got out of there right away."

"Good for her. But men like this one, they think that if they want something that it should be theirs. My name is Aisha McCade, by the way. And this is my son, Kenton. You've met Jorden." Gavin said nothing. "If you would put the gun down, I'd feel so much better."

"I can't put it down, Mrs. McCade. My mom told me that this thing might be the only thing between her seeing me alive again or in the morgue. I don't want her to come see me there. I've had a really hard time what with missing her, and I'd really hate to disappoint her by getting my butt shot up.'" Mom told Gavin of course he didn't want to disappoint her. "My grannie, I think she died. If it gets out that she is gone and her name, then they'll know that I'm here."

"Do you know who they are? The men that your mom is being chased by? Do you know them? Have you seen them lately?" Jorden wasn't sure who could be coming now, but they'd been warned that someone would. And if Gavin had any information they could use, it might help them. "Have you seen them since you and your mom separated?"

"No. And I can't call her either to let her know what's happened. The dragon, he said that it would be too dangerous. Mom said that determined people could track a fly fart if they thought it would give them what they wanted." Gavin flushed brightly. "I'm sorry. I'm really tired and hungry. Do you think you can tell me if my grannie is really gone? I need to figure out what I have to do next. Like where to live, and find something to eat."

"Yes, I can go now. But for as much as I'd like for you to stay here, I think it would be better if you came along with me. Just in case the owner might question why I'm there." Gavin sat down, his poor little body just giving up. When Kenton went to him to see if he was all right, Jorden noticed that he didn't bother trying to take his weapon. He wasn't sure if that was smart or not, but it wasn't pointed at any of them now, and Jorden thought he could live with that.

The hotel was within walking distance of his building. Kenton went in first with Gavin. Jorden stayed outside, just waiting while his mom went to get Gavin something to eat. He wasn't sure what to say to the kid, not having a lot of experience with them, but when Kenton came out of the room shaking his head, Gavin simply crumbled. Jorden was glad to have been closest to him to gather him in his arms while he dealt with his grief.

Jorden held him while he sobbed. He kept saying he was all alone now and that he wanted his mom. Jorden didn't blame him…right now he wanted his own. But when she showed up with a burger, fries, and a cola, Gavin said he wasn't hungry.

"You have to eat, kid. You want to get sick and end up somewhere you don't want to be? Someplace that you can't control? Like a hospital or something?" Gavin just looked at him—glared was more like it—and Jorden was impressed. Then Gavin told him he was already where he didn't want to be. "Yeah, okay, I'll give you that one. But eat and we'll get this figured out. My brother, Dalton, is coming by. He wants to talk to you too."

"How many brothers do you have?" Jorden told him five. "Sheesh. I bet they're all as big as you and Dr. McCade too. I guess if the bad guys are coming, it would be best if you weren't puny little guys like me."

"Yes, we're all pretty big men." Jorden snagged a fry and ate it as he continued. "Dalton is a cop, so don't freak out on him if he starts asking you cop questions. To be honest, I'm not sure that Dalton knows any other way to ask questions. Anyway, as you know, Kenton is a doctor. Private practice now. I paint. Grady fancies himself some sort of computer wizard, which really he is, but he works for this asshole that sort of takes advantage of him. Lewis, the baby, is a chef…a pretty good one, I guess, since he's got all these awards for his cooking. He lived with me until a little while ago, so I'm thinking he'll be finding him a place to put his hat. And Vance is…. Well, Vance is Vance. He has a job that pays well, but I'm

19

not entirely sure what it is he does any more. He was in the service until recently, and has been known to disappear from time to time."

Jorden told himself he wasn't babbling but biding his time until Gavin finished his meal. Besides, he was going to be staying with them now, so he needed to have the scoop on all of them.

By the time Kenton had made arrangements to have the body removed, Jorden and Gavin had moved back from the place and into the diner across the street. He hadn't wanted to leave, but Kenton explained to him that they were going to Jane Doe his grandma so that her name would never come out, and he had to keep a low profile. And if the press showed up, which was highly likely, they didn't want his picture taken.

In the end, Jorden took him to his house. By the time they were pulling up in front, not only had Gavin fallen asleep, but Jorden had spoken to Kenton and his mom twice about him. Jorden was glad now that he'd hired himself a staff. The house was fucking huge for a single man, but the kid was going to need someone to cook and clean up after him. Jorden hadn't the slightest idea what to do with a ten-year-old, but he liked him and figured they could work something out.

CHAPTER 2

Emma wasn't positive what to do with all her spare time. And this gardening stuff wasn't doing anything for her but give her a pounding headache. Going to the garden to see what was in the plot to match the picture books that she was using to figure out what was an herb and what ones were weeds wasn't helping either. She liked using fresh herbs when she cooked, but who knew they were this much work? When a shadow fell over her, she looked up from her book and smiled at Jorden and Gavin.

"I have to go into town to look at a shipment. It wasn't supposed to arrive until sometime next week, but it's here now. So I might be a little late, as there are two boxes of things that I didn't order. I don't think." She nodded to Jorden, who looked out of his element. "Gavin said that he doesn't mind staying at the house by himself, but I do. Maxwell and Abby are off today, so he'd be really alone in the house. I don't suppose you could keep an eye on him for me? Just until I can get things squared away for a sitter or something. Do ten year olds need sitters? I have no idea."

Gavin rolled his eyes but said nothing. She had had the pleasure of talking to him a little last night when they'd gone to Jorden's house to talk to the young man. He'd been quiet and polite, but he had also been overwhelmed. Emma knew just how he felt. She told Jorden that he could stay with her and not to worry about him.

When Jorden left them, she moved her project to the umbrella table near the garden plot. As much as she wanted to quit, she was determined to name at least four of the weeds or herbs in her garden before she did anything else. Gavin joined her at the table, but still hadn't said anything.

She had several leaves of the things she had found in the garden spread out in front of her. Three books were stacked up, as well as the open one in front of them. Emma thought she looked like a loon, or like she was going to conduct some kind of cooking experiment that involved a mishmash of everything. When he asked her what she was doing, Emma smiled at him.

"I'm trying my best to figure out if I have to start over in my garden here or if I have what I need for the kitchen. I don't suppose you know anything about herbs." He said only what he'd read. "More than I know, then. It's hard to figure out from a picture what things are, isn't it? I think this is marjoram, but I'm not sure."

He touched his fingers to the tiny leaf and took it to his nose. When he sneezed, she laughed and told him that she'd done that a lot over the last few hours. Wendell, the cook, came out with not just tall glasses of iced tea, but a plate of her cookies as well. Emma offered them to Gavin.

"It's oregano, not marjoram. Can be used for the same dishes, but oregano is stronger and has less of a bite to it." She set it aside and marked it on her Post-it notes. He picked up the next herb she was clueless about. "Nasturtium. You can eat all of this plant, including the flower and the leaves. Do you suppose that the people coming here for Mom will hurt you guys too?"

Emma paused in writing the name of the plant down and looked at Gavin before speaking. "Yes. I mean, I don't know that they'll hurt us, but they'll try. They did when I got here with the ring. Mostly it was my mother; she wasn't a nice person, but there are others, the dragon told us. There was a lot going on that had nothing to do with the ring really, just a lot of greedy people making it harder on everyone."

Gavin nodded and picked up the horseradish that she'd been able to identify. When he said nothing more, she handed him two more little leaves. One she was sure was peppermint, the other something like it but sweeter.

"This is peppermint, but this is chocolate mint. I guess people can put them in ice cubes and then in tea. I don't think I'd care for that." Emma nodded then took him to the area she was working in. "You've got most of them. Lambs ear is an old herb used during wars to soften the bandages on the soldiers. You should plant some marigolds around your garden to keep the pests out."

"I will. How do you know so much about herbs?" Gavin said nothing but did sit down in the dirt and start pulling weeds. Emma watched what he was leaving compared to pulling, and decided that she needed more help than a book. Sitting next to him, she noticed that his shoes were new, as was the rest of his clothing. Jorden had been shopping, apparently.

"I'm smart. Like off the charts smart. Mom had me in this special school, but I had to leave there after the money from my dad's estate stopped coming in. I know she tried to make the payments, but it was just too much." Emma said nothing.

"I don't tell her anymore how bored I am in school. She cried at night, and that hurt me all the way to my core."

"I know that to be considered genius you have to score at least a one forty. You said off the charts. What is your score, Gavin?" He pulled several more things out of the ground. Emma had a feeling he was trying to figure out if she'd believe him or not and changed the subject. "When I first moved into this house, Kenton had no table and chairs and only a mattress on the floor. While I was thrilled to have a lovely home like this, I fell in love with the kitchen. You see, I love to cook and he lets me."

"I doubt that anyone lets you do anything, Mrs. McCade. You seem like you just go ahead and do what you want." She wasn't sure if he was being rude or not; it was still hard for her to tell sometimes when someone complimented her. "My mom is like that. She's really mouthy at times, Grannie says... said. But I love her, so I don't get in her way when she gets like she can."

"She take on someone that you were having trouble with?" He nodded and stared at the tree line. "I'm betting that she was all over them about it, too. And she didn't like the way it made her feel afterwards either."

"No, she didn't. Mom is a wonderful person, but she gets all intense when she's upset. She told me later that she wished that she'd been calmer, dealt with the teacher better, but all I could think about was how protective she was and how proud I was of her for standing up to the guy." Emma asked him what the teacher had done. "When I was tested for how smart I was, he was the proctor. There were several of us in the room taking the test, but I didn't screw off like they did. I took the test, and then when I was done, I got up and laid it next to him. He'd fallen asleep, you see, and he felt that someone, namely me, should have awakened him at some point. I didn't think that was my responsibility; and besides, when I do things like that, I get labeled as a nerd. Thanks but no thanks, I guess."

"I see. And since you'd done so well, he figured that you'd cheated. And even if he didn't think that, it was a way to get back at you. He sounds like a shit." He nodded. "The other kids, did they score as well? I'm betting not."

"No. Not as well. Good, but not as well. I scored a perfect. No one else came close to that." When he continued to stare at the tree line, she looked too. There were deer there, several of them, as well as a wolf. Emma knew he wasn't wild, but one of the pack that roamed the area for Kenton. "When I was asked to take the test again, this time at the college, he was there again. This time.... He should have known there were cameras in the room with us, I think. And when he laid his head down and fell asleep, I simply finished my test and left the room like I had before. And since I was the only one taking the retest and he was being watched, he got caught. When he woke up.... He wasn't a nice person."

"Did he change your answers? Why that fucking bastard. Where is he? Someone needs to teach him—" Gavin laughed, and she smiled back at him. "I'm a little protective of you as well, I guess. Did the little shit lose his job?"

"He did, and his nose was broken and he had to get stitches in his forehead when he hit the wall behind him." Emma laughed. "Like I said, when she gets that way, I get out of her way. I would suggest that anyone should if she's on a path."

They worked for a bit more before she invited him inside to have something to eat. Kenton had told her this morning that he'd be home early, and they were going to have a light dinner then go see a movie. She wasn't sure what he'd want to do now that they had company. But when he came in the house, he acted like it wasn't any big deal to have a kid changing their plans, and had Gavin help set the table for them. Emma started on dinner for them while the two of them talked.

"I've had a long conversation with Dragon today. By the way, your mom is aware that you're here and that her grandma passed away. Dragon told her for us. She also said to tell you that she was coming as soon as she got some money." Emma asked if they could send her some. "No. If we do, they'll be all over it. She'd have to show some sort of identification to pick it up, and her driver's license would give her away. We have a feeling that they're just waiting for someone to claim to be her, and then it'll be over. Dragon has a plan, he told me, to help her get here. She needs money and he's going to help her get it."

Emma wasn't sure that she wanted to know, but Gavin did. And when Kenton told him that what she was doing was illegal but her only means of getting here, she could tell that he was upset about it. Kenton told Gavin that he thought she was a good person and had had bad things happen to her, so this was the only way to help her.

"She won't like it, and if she's agreed, then she must be scared." Kenton just glanced at Emma. Whatever had happened, he'd tell her later. "Do you know who gets the earrings when she gets here? I'm guessing that like the ring, it goes to one of you guys."

"Yes. But that's not how it works with this. We don't take whatever is brought to us, Gavin. Your mom won't be able to remove them, just as Emma wasn't. Nor will she be able to leave once she's here." He nodded but stared at his burger when Kenton continued. "Like Emma, she's a part of the dragon, and when your mom meets with one of my brothers, to be his mate, then she'll live with him."

Gavin didn't say much for the rest of the meal. He wasn't rude, but she could tell that some of his good mood from earlier had somehow gotten sucked out of him. When she asked him if he wanted any cake, he declined and asked if he could just read. The library was opened for him and he sat in one of the big overstuffed chairs when he found something. Emma wasn't surprised to see that he'd picked a book well beyond his age.

As she and Wendell were cleaning up, she tried to think what might have saddened Gavin. Emma thought for sure he'd be happy to know that his mom was coming here, but he was depressed. When Kenton told her that Jorden was on his way, she nodded, distracted.

"He said that he's eaten." Again, Emma nodded. "He also stopped off and had sex with nine hookers before he got in his truck and ran them down. I think there might be an inquiry about it, but you know Jorden, he can charm his way out of most anything."

"I'm sure that he used a condom and hopefully he can get the blood off his truck before coming here. And for the record, I'm paying attention to you, but I'm also thinking. It is possible to do both." He pulled her into his arms. "What happened at dinner? We had a lot of fun this evening, and now he looks so sad."

"Maybe he got to thinking of his grannie and it hurt him." Could be, she thought, but Emma didn't think that was it. It had to do with his mom coming here. "Jorden has spent the most time with him, perhaps he can get it out of him."

Emma wasn't sure it was going to be any easier for Jorden. Whatever was going on in Gavin's head, he'd let them know

27

when he was ready. Or, she thought, when he figured it out on his own.

~~~

Jasmine sat in the chair, but said nothing to the groups around her. Her grannie had died, and she'd not been there with her when she had. When the announcer said that the next race was up, Jasmine didn't even bother looking at the tickets in her hand. So far the dragon had predicted every horse race correctly, and she was pretty sure she was going to have more than enough to get to her little boy. Maybe she'd have enough to get him some new shoes. His old ones were sort of worn out.

When we have finished here, perhaps it would be a good time for you to go to the little shop and purchase a bag to put your things in. She told him she'd do that. Not that she had all that much to put in the bag; everything she'd had after sending Gavin to the McCades was now in a dumpster, no doubt. She'd read about the break-in at the hotel yesterday where she'd been staying. When the men hadn't been able to find her at the auction, they had gone back to her hotel and trashed it. Everything she had had been destroyed.

She was glad now that she'd not used her actual name when checking in, not that it had done much good, apparently. But somehow they'd found her resting place and had destroyed the few things that she'd had with her, and even the room. She'd hate to have to pay the bill for that damage. The place looked like a bomb had gone off in it from the pictures that she'd seen on the news. Jasmine wondered what they might have done had she been there. It was scary to think about.

My lady? She told the dragon that she just needed a minute. *The race is over. It is time that we move on. Once you have made your purchases, we'll take the tickets and claim your winnings.*

28

Standing up, she tensed when he told her to stand very still. He'd told her just this morning that the people were looking for her harder now, so she would need to do whatever he told her when he did. She wondered if it was because they were getting desperate or that she was getting that good at hiding from them. Whatever it was, she was terrified out of her mind. So when he said that things were back to normal, she did have a moment of terror, wondering if things would ever be normal again.

Making a stop at the gift shop, she picked out a bag that the dragon suggested, as well as a ball cap for Gavin. Picking up a couple of candy bars, about the only thing she could keep down with all this stress, she made her way to the claim counter. It was silly, she knew, to get him a ball cap to a place neither of them would ever go to again. But she wanted to hold it to her tonight when she went to bed. Jasmine missed Gavin so much she ached with it.

Standing in line with her winning tickets, she asked Dragon how she was traveling from here. Her body was worn out, and she no longer cared if what she was doing was wrong or not. Just getting the gun on the plane with her grannie had been hard enough. For Dragon, making everyone in the line believe that it was a hairdryer and not a handgun had drained him a little too, he'd told her. As soon as the plane was in the air, she'd had to go into hiding again, fearful that even being at the big airport would alert the bad guys to where her family was going.

Her turn in the long line at the cashier was next, and she handed over the tickets to the man behind the glass. He made a comment about her having a good day and she only smiled. Jasmine had done just what Dragon told her to do, filling out the betting sheets with each mark that he said. Not that she had any idea what she was doing, but it must have worked. When the man asked her if she wanted an escort, Jasmine told him no, she was fine, and he asked her for the bag. Not sure what was going on, she handed it over, telling him she had a receipt.

"I can see it there. You're all right, little lady."

When he turned his back on her, she panicked a little. But the dragon told her it was fine, he could tell that this man was honest. When he turned back to her, handing her bag back to her through a special door, she took it and nearly fell with the weight. As she walked away, Jasmine tried to think how long she'd been here and what he'd put in the bag. Jasmine asked the dragon if he'd made the cashier give her more than she'd won.

No. I would not cheat the man that way. He would lose his job should he do that. What you have there, it is yours, all of it. Jasmine asked him how much they'd won. *I do not know money as well as I should. But you have enough. Should you perhaps just go to the dealership now to get a car?*

I don't know. I have to see what I have here. After figuring that out, I'll be able to think how best to use it to get to my son. He told her again it was enough, he was sure. *Yet you don't know money well. For all I know I could have won a thousand dollars and he paid me all in ones.*

Jasmine went into the bathroom and the first empty stall. Putting the heavy bag on the baby holder behind the door, she unzipped the thing and looked inside. When she saw what was in it, she staggered back. There was a lot more than ones in the bag, and a hell of a lot more than just a thousand dollars. She asked the dragon again how much was in here as she stood up and peered into the bag once more.

As I have said, I do not know money well. But you have one million seventy-one thousand, seven hundred forty-three dollars in there. That will be enough to get you transportation, won't it? She nodded, then told him it was more than enough. *Good. I'm very glad. I did have the man think it wasn't necessary to report your winnings. I think that would bring us more trouble than we need at the moment.*

You could be right. One million seventy-one thousand seven hundred forty-three dollars. It was more money than she'd seen in all her life. And she'd won it at the races. *Was it necessary for me to win this much? And I'm pretty sure that you know that anything over a hundred grand is a lot of money.*

I did not want you to have to do without when it came to Gavin and his school after you get back to him. She felt her tears fall. *You have said to me that you wish you could afford to give him a better education. It is something that he enjoyed very much. I wanted to help you with that. Was it wrong of me?*

No. Not for him it's not. Had it been for, I don't know, just me, I would have had you give it back or something, but I'll use this for him. For my son's education when this is done. She took out several one hundred dollar bills and some of the smaller denominations and put them in her wallet. *I have to think. I'm going to go out and find a place to eat and think.*

Jasmine had to think what she needed to do now. And in what sort of order. Getting to Ohio was first and foremost, but there had to be steps taken to get her there. Clothing for sure, transportation, and she needed to make sure that she was safe while doing it and once she was there. And that she was not followed, to keep Gavin safe.

The first thing she did was go to a Walmart. Clothing. It took her longer than she thought it would to find some cheap clothing. Since she had nothing, she had to basically start from scratch, from the underthings to everything on the outside.

Shoes too, as well as a small first aid kit. If she got hurt, she wanted to be able to make it so she'd not bleed to death. By the time she was done, Jasmine was exhausted again. Taking a cab to the nearest hotel wasn't expensive, but she had to start watching every penny. She couldn't very well pull open her bag with horses all over the side of it and pull some out whenever she was short.

The cheap hotel didn't ask for any form of identification, for which she was grateful. After getting in her room, Jasmine not only locked the door but moved the dresser in front of it as well. Then Jasmine took a shower. Being clean for the first time in a couple of days felt like heaven, and she lingered in the water for a bit longer than she normally would have, simply because she could.

After she ordered a pizza, terrified that the kid bringing it to her would be toting a gun, she ate it as she laid out what she had. It wasn't much, but it was enough to get her going. Then she went to the ads in the paper of someone selling a used car.

Did you not want new, my lady? I thought that it would be more reliable for you and Gavin once you were with the McCades. Jasmine wasn't going to stay with them and told the dragon again. *But you must. Without you there, I will not be complete.*

You'll just have to wing it then. I have to get my son safe. He's all I have in the world now, and he has to come first over you and your dragon. She circled two cars that she thought might do. *Besides, I can't just go into a dealership and lay down forty grand for a new car and not have someone ask me questions. I wouldn't even know how to answer them. I'm sure that telling them that a dragon in my head talked to the horses or whatever and asked them to win will go over well. Oh, and what do I tell them when they ask why I needed to buy a car with cash? How do you think that will go over when I tell them that I have these pretty earrings that madmen want, and they'll kill me for them should I stick around here for very long?*

I only looked into the horses' minds and encouraged them a bit. Nothing more than that. And you made me promise not to do that again so I cannot help you with the car now. Jasmine said nothing. It was cheating no matter how anyone looked at it. *You will be home soon. I, for one, am excited to see which young man you awaken the dragon in.*

He would be, she supposed. But instead of getting into another argument with him on the McCades, Jasmine went to bed. Tomorrow was going to be another very long day.

But instead of falling asleep like she really needed to, she thought about the turns in her life since she'd gotten the earrings. Why, her mind kept asking her, was it her and not the sixty or so others at that auction? Any one of them could have carried these things to the McCades. Why had she not just given them to the man in the first place when he'd obviously wanted them?

And this man, the one she was supposedly to be paired with, what on earth would that be like should she stay? A nightmare, she knew it. She and men did not get along. Her grannie had told her often enough it was because she'd not found the right one. Well, one mistake was enough, thanks. But she'd gotten Gavin out of that marriage, and that was all she'd ever really needed. Her husband, Kris Tyler, had been a nice enough man, just not for her. Or any woman. Jasmine supposed the damage to her heart had been done because she really had loved him.

Kris hadn't been a bad man, not really. He had tried to make her happy right up until the honeymoon. But he had married her under false pretenses, and she could never forgive him for that. Had it not been for their wedding night and Gavin coming from that, she would have been just fine in divorcing him and living alone. But the day they left for their honeymoon, while still on the plane to Paris, he told her his reasons for pursuing her so hard.

"I'm gay." She nodded, then shook her head. "I am. I married you — not that I don't care for you — but I married you so that I could inherit my mom's estate. And I will take care of you, I promise. Mom said that without a wife, I couldn't get anything. I know that sounds like I'm a greedy bastard, but I had to do something. But being married to you, it's not what I wanted. You're nice, but not what I need to make me happy. Please, Jasmine, don't be angry."

"I'll be angry if I damned well want to. You don't love me, yet you married me." He shook his head no, and said again that he cared for her but he didn't love her. "Care for me. You care for me? How is that supposed to keep me...? We had sex. You and I had sex last night."

She realized her voice had gotten louder when he turned red and looked around. Jasmine hadn't cared. She was going on her honeymoon, to Paris, with a man who didn't love her and never would. Being angry wasn't even close to what she was feeling.

"Yes, we did. I knew that I'd have to at least once in a while, but I don't think I can do that again." Her heart, already tender from his admission, shattered at his words. "I know I should have said something earlier, but I was afraid that you'd say no."

"You're damned right I would have said no. Kris, I love you." He nodded and leaned back on his seat, saying nothing. "Is there someone else? Another person?"

"Another man. Yes, there is. And he is meeting me in Paris. He and I are going to spend our lives together, but I promise you, we'll provide for you for as long as you want."

Her honeymoon, her first trip abroad, had been a ruse as well. A nice way for Donald and Kris to have a good time while she.... Jasmine had never been sure what she was supposed to do while they honeymooned. So, just after the plane landed, she was filing for a flight back home and making plans to get her life back to normal.

Of course Kris's mom had found out, and had cut him out of the will and her life. Kris had stayed with Jasmine then... he'd had nowhere else to go. Even Donald, his longtime lover, had left him in pursuit of a man with money and a home that didn't have a wife and kid in it. Apparently when Kris promised to take care of her, Donald had thought that they'd be living in the big house, with her someplace else.

Mrs. Tyler had made her life a living hell when it was obvious that Gavin was Kris's son. She wanted her grandson to raise as her own, because to her Kris was dead. Beth went to great lengths, even trying to claim that Jasmine was a poor mother and that her grandson deserved more. And when Jasmine refused to give him up to her, Beth had gone out of her way to ruin her. And nearly had. She'd lost her house, her car, and could no longer afford Gavin's daycare while she worked. Because no matter what job she had, Beth would fuck it up for her. Finally, she'd had to move in with her grannie and help her with the bills while she watched Gavin during her shifts. And when Beth died, after seven long years of abuse to her and Kris, she filed for divorce. As far as she was concerned there was no more reason for her to be married to Kris. His mom hadn't changed her mind and it needed to be over.

Jasmine had hurt for Kris; he was just a man, trying to be loved, and his mom had fucked that up for him. Not that Donald might have been the right man, but no matter who he found, she'd ruin it for him. Elizabeth Tyler was a mean, selfish bitch, and Jasmine had hated her with a passion. When she'd passed away, Jasmine had actually done a little jig. Of course it had been in her room where no one could see her. She wasn't that heartless.

Then a short week after the decree had come through that she was no longer married to him, Kris had been found dead, a note of why he couldn't live any longer beside him, along with a letter to Gavin. Whatever had been in the letter to his son, Jasmine had no idea. But Gavin read it, and as far as she knew, he still had it. It was between just the two of them.

Life after that had never taken an uphill turn. No matter what she tried or did, everything seemed to be one major failure after another. Until she started flipping things on the Internet and going to auctions. They'd been starting to be able to put a little away. Then she found the earrings.

CHAPTER 3

Jorden looked around his new studio. He'd been moving in for over a month now, and was finally as finished as he could be. The five story building had seemed too much when he'd gotten started, but now he liked the way it was set up, and the fact that he had more room than he'd hoped for. He grinned at Gavin when he came out of the storage room with dirt and dust on his face. He'd been helping him every day since he'd been with him.

"You been mopping up the floor with your head? You have more dust on you than I think I have on the floor to the pottery room." The kid had been a tremendous help over the last few days. Not just in getting things settled in here, but he had staved off the loneliness of living in his own home. "I've been thinking that we should go and have dinner in town tonight. How about pizza or burgers?"

"Pizza sounds really good, but are you going to order that wimpy kind? Because if you are, then we might as well have burgers." Jorden grinned wider. The kid had a taste for hot and spicy, even more so than his brother, Grady. "Oh wait, you told Kenton that we'd go by there and see him after we were done here."

"I already spoke to him, and since Emma is working on the charity thing with my mom, we men are going to get together." Gavin still got nervous around his brothers. He hadn't figured out why yet, but he knew that he preferred them one at a time. "We can just go to my house after picking something up if you want."

"I'm going to miss you guys." It was the second time today that he'd said something like that. The first time was when he'd offered to pay him for working with him. Gavin had said that the money would come in handy when he was gone. Then this.

"Are you going somewhere that I don't know about? I mean, from what I've heard from Dragon, your mom should be here within the next few days. Are you taking off before she gets here?" Gavin said no but didn't elaborate. "Gavin, what's this about? The other day Emma said that you were upset about something, and when I asked you, you told me it was all right. It's not all right. We're friends. What's up?"

"When my mom gets here, one of you are going to take her as your mate, right? I had to ask around to figure out what that meant, but I'm guessing she'll be like a wife to one of you." Jorden nodded, not sure where this was going. "Then there is me. I don't know what I'm supposed to do. I guess.... What about me, Jorden? What if one of you guys take her and decide that I'm not your kid and tell her that I have to go? She might do it if she is happy, don't you think? I mean...I don't know what I'll do, but I sure am going to miss you guys."

Jorden was shocked. Did the kid actually think that they'd just...? A lot of things came to mind that had been going on in that moment. It wasn't that he was afraid of his brothers, he was trying his best to distance himself from them. He didn't want to spend time with his mom for the same reasons. There was the way that he'd never unpacked. No matter how many times Jorden had told him it was fine to use the big dressers and closet in his room, Gavin would put his things back in the shopping bag as if he was ready to go all the time. Jorden asked him to have a seat.

"First of all, I don't think that any of my brothers, Kenton included, would tell you that you had to go. They all love you." Gavin said nothing. Jorden sometimes forgot that he was only ten for all his smarts, and had been through a great deal in the last few months. "Secondly, I think my mom would take you as her own son over one of us if it ever came to that. Not that it would, but she loves you so much."

"She told me I was nicer to her than you boys are. I don't think she's taken a good look at you guys lately. I'm a boy, you guys are big men. And not a one of you would do a thing to upset her. I think you're all afraid of her, aren't you?" Jorden nodded and laughed. "I like Mrs. McCade. And she has this pretty great house too. I know you lived there and all, but did you know that she can sing all kinds of old music? And she has a turntable with all these amazing albums that she lets me listen to. She's about the coolest lady I've ever met."

"You should tell her that. She'd love it. And I do know about the albums. Anytime that we're all together for holidays or whatever, she puts it out on the back deck and we all listen to it. Over and over and over." Gavin laughed. "No one is going to ask you to leave. There is not one person here that wouldn't do just about anything for you. Emma said that you've helped her with her garden, and she's using the herbs now when she is cooking. Mom told me that you fixed her computer when none of us could. Not to mention, the way you've got me all organized here, I'm going to be working again a lot sooner than I thought I'd be when I started this."

"But that wasn't that much. What if one of your brothers or even you want their own kid? What will they do with me?"

Jorden wanted to tell him that wouldn't happen, but he pulled the kid into his arms instead. "You can come and stay with me. Forever if you want. But really, I don't even think that is a possibility. Even Lewis, who is the baby of this family, said that he could not wait for you to call him Uncle, or even Dad should it come to that." Gavin said he had already asked him if he would. "See? They love you as much as I do."

Gavin looked up at him, and Jorden could see that he really wanted to trust him. To believe what he was saying was true. But he was cautious, something he'd learned the boy was very good at. He supposed it had a lot to do with his own father, someone that had been out of his life more than in. Nor did he think that his father had understood the boy. Jorden just listened to him, had a blast with the kid, and decided that he'd love a kid just like him someday. Gavin's own father, Kris Tyler, had missed a lot being the man that he was.

Jorden had done a background check on not just Gavin's mom, but the entire family. Gavin's father hadn't been a good dad to him. And his grandma, his dad's mother, a woman that should have been shot long ago as far as Jorden could see, was a mean, manipulative woman who had cut off her only son in favor of wanting someone normal. To her, Kris Tyler being a homosexual had made him unworthy of her love or money. It was really too bad that she couldn't see that for him to be what he was, was normal for him. Sad, but Jorden thought there were a great many people in the world like her, and would be forever. Idiots who didn't understand that you couldn't help who you loved or who loved you.

I just heard from Dragon; Jasmine has been in an accident. Jorden didn't say anything to Gavin, but asked Kenton if she was all right. *Yes. A little beat up, but for the most part, doing well. Emma and I are going to go and pick her up. She's about an hour from here. Do you want to come along with Gavin? Might do her some good to see him.*

I'd love to, but I'll find out what Gavin wants to do. I think he's a lot like his mom when it comes to having people tell him what he's going to be doing instead of asking him what he might want. Kenton laughed. *Come on by the studio, and I'll have an answer by the time you get here. Any details that I can tell him?*

No. Not that we have much. She's hurt but not critically. The car she was driving was hit from the side, and lucky for her there was a cop close by or there is no telling what they might have done to her when they got out of their SUV. He said he might have more questions than he had answers for, and Kenton told him he had a little too. *Also, you might prepare him. She's pretty rattled, Dragon said.*

Jorden said he would handle it. Pulling the boy from him, he looked into his eyes. He was almost afraid to tell him that his mom had been hurt, but he also knew that he deserved to know it all. He was a good kid, smart, and if he only got part of what had happened, his mind would put in things that wasn't there. So he told him that Kenton was coming to get them and why.

"Is she going to die?" Jorden told him what Kenton had said. "But it was someone trying to kill her, right? They're after her still."

"Yes. For whatever reason that we can't get from the dragon, people want to stop her from coming here. Money could be a part of it. We know that there are groups trying to get all the pieces together before we do, but he said he knows very little." Gavin nodded and asked if they were going there now. "Yes. I can go if you want me to, but—"

The hug was unexpected but powerful. Jorden hugged him back, feeling it all over his body and well into his heart. Gavin cried for five minutes, long enough for Kenton to come in the room then leave, giving him the privacy that the boy needed. When he seemed to have some control over his emotions, he told Jorden he was very sorry.

"There is no reason to be sorry, Gavin. I don't know what I'd do if something happened to my mom. And with the fact that you've had all this other shit going on too, it's no wonder that you have a moment or two of pain." Gavin asked him if he'd go too. "Yes. If you want. I would never assume anything."

"She might be mouthy. I know I told you that before, but when she's hurting, she has no filter." He asked him how often she got hurt. "Not too much. But once when she was helping one of her clients move a pie safe in her house, Mom told her that she had it. But the lady wanted to help. Mom said that she felt she needed to, to be not thought of as old. Anyway, she shoved when Mom was too close, and she smashed her hand all up in the doorframe. Mrs. Dunlap, she sure did get red in the face when Mom started cursing. And she can do that like it's her job."

They were both laughing as they made their way out of the building. As he locked up, Jorden thought of the woman that he'd come to admire without meeting her. He wondered which of his brothers she'd be mated to, and was somewhat jealous. She might be a lot of fun to be with.

~~~

Jasmine tried her best not to scream when the nurse, a little bit of a girl, tried to stitch up her arm. Christ, were the meds never going to kick in? When the curtain was thrown back, Jasmine just knew it was the bad guys again and tensed up. But the cop standing there wasn't much better. The prick had been talking to her like she was nothing but a hooker on the run for the last hour. Every time he opened his mouth, she wanted to shove something into it, like her fist.

"We got some more questions for you." Jasmine just looked at the nurse and willed her not to leave her alone with the man. "You ready to tell me what I want to know, or are you gonna try that crap again about not knowing anything?"

"I don't know what you're talking about." She was glad now that she'd put all her money in the locker she'd rented at the bus station. She was pretty sure that Joe Blow here, whatever his name really was, would have had a shit fit if he'd found it. A million in cash without any means of showing where it came from would have just made his day, she thought.

Dragon had told her she was close to the McCades' home, and that within the hour she would be there. Jasmine had decided that putting the money somewhere she could grab it and go would be better than having to explain to the family why she had it. Also, if they tried any shit, she was going to need it to run. With her son.

"You said you didn't know the vehicle that hit you. But when we searched the car after he took off, there were several pictures of you in the glove box." That terrified her more than she could think around. "Some kid too. You know him?"

He handed her two plastic bags, evidence bags it said on them, and she looked at the one of her first. It was taken recently, when she'd been at the grocery store getting snacks for the road. The other one, of Gavin, was older, by a couple of years. She handed them back to the man and said she didn't know why they'd have those.

"I think I've wasted enough time on you, Jasmine. That is your name, isn't it? Where is he? Where is Gavin?" That question startled her and she jerked her arm just as the nurse was sticking her again. Looking at the cop, Jasmine had a feeling that she was not going to make it out of here alive. And when the drug started oozing through her head, she watched as the man pulled out a gun and shot the nurse with it. "Less people that I have to share my ill-gotten gains with." The laughter after he spoke seemed to vibrate in her head.

Things started moving at different speeds after that. The bullet seemed to leave the gun at a super slow speed when he aimed at her and fired. Then she could hardly see the gun at all, the way it moved fast like a dark blur. Voices were louder too, like they were shouting at her right at her ear, but she couldn't make the words out as they were slurred.

The curtain surrounding her and the cop was torn from the hooks slowly, one at a time, and the sound of it was like a pop, pop, pop noise. A movement of colors, blues and golds, took her breath away. Not sure what it was, she reached out to touch it, only to find herself on the floor looking up at the bottom of the bed. The dead nurse stared at her from her position beside her. The blood from her head seeping out around her looked surreal, like Jasmine was watching a movie. Looking up when she heard her name, she thought it was Gavin but couldn't make her mouth work to ask him what he was doing there.

"Jasmine, can you hear me?" She tore her eyes from her son and looked at the big man beside her. The movement made her sick, so she closed her eyes. "You have to stay awake for me, Jasmine. Did they give you anything? For pain or something?"

"Needle, whatever was in it made me sick." She turned her head and felt herself being lifted up when she got sick. Twice she threw up and had to close her eyes again. "I don't know what it was. But I think it might be trying to kill me."

"We're going to move you, all right? Gavin is here with me, and he's going to get your things. Do you have a purse? Bag? Dragon said that you have a bag stashed somewhere."

Like she'd trust him with that information. The man laughed and told her she could. Jasmine hadn't realized she'd spoken aloud until then. She tried to focus on him, anyone really, and it made her sick again. She asked the man who he was.

"My name is Jorden, Jorden McCade. Gavin has been staying with me for a few days. I know you heard about your grandmother, so I had Gavin stay with me until you got here." She nodded, and then grabbed her head when it felt like it was going to fall off. "My brother, Kenton, he and Emma are going to take care that no one knows we were here once you are out of here. The cop, did you know him?"

"Did?" He told her yes, did. "I see. So something or someone killed him. Good. I think he might have been trying to kill me too. He was working with the nurse. Said something about less money to be shared, or something like that. Just before he shot her in the head."

"I'm sure of it. Come on now, I'm going to set you on the bed. Do you have clothing here?" When she was sitting on the side of the bed, she felt her head roll forward. Pointing in the general direction of the little closet next to her, she saw her son again. Gavin really was here. "Your shirt is all bloodied. I'm going to just pull this off you, all right? I'd say we could leave it on you, but I'm afraid that it's not in good shape."

She wanted it off her too. There wasn't just her blood on

45

it, she'd bet, and helped him pull it over her head. Jasmine wasn't sure why she felt he'd not take advantage of her, but she felt.... Well, she felt safe. For the first time in a long while.

"I was sideswiped at an intersection where I had the right of way. Then when I get here, this cop, who was first on the scene, he shows me pictures of myself and Gavin. But he knows us. I think they're trying to find me." Jorden said he knew that. It was why he was here. "I just want to hand over the jewelry and go away. I need to just rest. Take my son and just go away."

"We've got you now."

His voice sounded so strong, like he really did have her. But men were trying to kill her, and if she hung around with these people, they'd try and kill them as well. Jasmine wasn't sure why she knew this, but she did. So when she closed her eyes again, just to get her head to stop spinning, Jasmine let whatever drugs were inside of her take her under.

Jasmine woke up feeling sick again, but safe. When she started to roll over to her side, her head began to spin and her belly lurched up. Closing her eyes again, she felt someone take her hand, and then she looked at her son. Gavin looked wonderful, and taking his hand to her mouth, she kissed it and then closed her eyes again. It was easier than being sick. But just knowing that he was close made all the difference in the world.

When she opened her eyes again she knew that she was no longer in the hospital. In fact, she was in a really nice bedroom with more antiques than she'd seen at auction houses. Trying not to move too quickly, she rolled to her back and felt someone beside her. Before she could figure out who it was, a soft light came on, barely showing the man sitting next to the bed.

"It's Gavin there. He wouldn't leave you now that you're

here." She nodded, then felt her belly jerk. "My brother, Kenton, is a doctor, and he checked on you once we got you home. He said that while you're going to be fine, the drug still needs to work its way out of your system. And that might take a few days. He said you were very lucky that the nurse hadn't been able to give you the entire dose before she was—"

"He killed her. That cop, he pulled out his gun and killed that girl." The man nodded but said nothing more. "He wasn't really a cop, was he? But someone that came to get me. And that nurse, she was on his payroll too, wasn't she?"

"Yes. He was a cop, but he was also there to kill you and take the earrings from you. The nurse, from what we can figure out, wasn't anyone that the staff knew. They think, like the cop, that she was on someone's payroll, as you said. Lucky for you and us, Dragon called out to Kenton as soon as the other vehicle hit you and we were already on our way. I'm to tell you that had you been in a smaller car, or even one that was newer, you wouldn't have survived." Jasmine put her hand on Gavin's head and felt better for that small touch. "There are no traces of you at the hospital, nothing to lead them here, nor to tell anyone that you had even been there. There were two calls put out on the cop's phone, and my brother is looking into who they might have gone to, but so far nothing. I'm telling you this so you know that we're doing everything we can to keep you and Gavin safe. And we will."

"Death to all dragons." He asked her what she meant. "It was a tat on the arm of a man I saw a few days ago. Dragon told me what it meant...I had no idea at the time. One of the men at the accident, he had it too, on his neck. I think they're part of the ones trying to kill me for the earrings. The dragon said the group name was old, something from the beginning of his time on Earth, but he didn't think this was the same group. They don't have the same agenda."

"I'll have Grady look into that for us." She told him it was written in Chinese. "Good to know. Also, I'm to ask you about the stash of money. Not that I want it, but if you took it to a locker, bus station or someplace like that, you might have been seen on cameras and that might not be good. Dragon told me that you might want to run with it."

"He's just a wealth of information, isn't he?" The man laughed. "I remember you telling me your name, but I don't remember what it is. I know that there were other people there, besides the nurse and cop, but for the life of me, all I can remember is streaks of gold and blue."

"Kenton. He's a dragon." Jasmine looked at the man. "I'm Jorden. And yes, you did have a lot going on, so it's small wonder that you don't remember me. I need to tell you a couple of things before Gavin wakes up, please."

"I don't think I want to know." He nodded. "You're going to tell me that this thing, this thing with the dragon and the jewelry, you're the man I'm to give it to. I think he called you a mate to me."

"That's right. When you were in the hospital I helped you dress. Touching your skin, even in the rush that we were in, I pulled your head to my chest to help redress you and I could smell you, feel what you were to me. The earrings, one of them, touched me. Nothing untoward, I promise you, but as soon as it did, I could feel changes in my body, and my dragon seemed to come alive for me." Jasmine said nothing to him as he continued. "I'm not saying that you need to look now, but you'll see it when you dress again. You have a mark on your skin, a dragon. Just as I do now."

He pulled his shirt from his pants and lifted it to above where his heart would be. Jasmine stared at his chest…not just the mark, but him. Christ, he was beautiful. He looked like he'd been carved from some stone then covered in skin. She wanted to touch him in the worst way. Jasmine looked at him when he said her name.

"I can smell you, everything about you." She pressed her legs together and felt her face heat up. "I'm sorry about this."

"It's fine. It's been a long time, is all." She turned to look at her son who still slept by her. "Gavin's dad wasn't really into me. He thought he could make it work, making love to me on occasion, but he told me that he just didn't want to be with me. I understand if you feel the same."

"What do you mean, you understand?" When she didn't answer him, he pulled her chin around so that she was looking at him. Jasmine wasn't afraid of him but she was aware of him, as a man. "What is it you think you understand about me? Or about what I need?"

"I'm not that much." He asked her much what. "A woman, I'm not much of a woman. And I'm not very nice either. When I see something that pisses me off, I tear into it without thinking about what I'm saying. Grannie used to tell me that my mouth was going to get me in serious crap one day, and she was right. Jorden, I know what I am."

"Apparently you don't."

When he pressed his mouth to hers, all she could think about was warmth, then when his tongue slipped into her mouth and tangled with her own, Jasmine felt her body not just wake up, but it seemed to take notice of every single thing about him. She could smell him, not just the cologne that he had on but the shampoo he'd used. His soap had a minty smell to it, and an underlying odor of paint. When he cupped the back of her head, tilting hers just a little, the kiss deepened. He took more but gave as well.

He touched more than her mouth with his. She felt his mind roll over hers, his thoughts become mingled with hers. And when she saw them together in this bed, she was naked, screaming out in pleasure as he ate her. Jasmine felt her body heat, warm to the thoughts of coming with him, having him take her to such heights, ones that she'd never felt before.

When he lifted his head, leaning his forehead onto hers, Jasmine could have sworn that she could hear his heart pounding. Or maybe it was hers. She could certainly feel it there, beating a mile a minute. Something had happened just now; not just a kiss, but it felt as if he'd branded her, claimed her in some way.

"You have no idea how much I'd like to do just what was in our minds right now."

Without thought as to what might happen, she moved her hand down his chest to his pants. When he cupped her hand in his, Jasmine watched as he took her hand to his cock and rocked into her palm. His moan made her feel sexy, like he desired her. And when he kissed her again, a quick touching of the mouths that left her no less devastated, she moaned as well. "The thought of tasting you, having you come down my throat before I take you deeply, has me aching."

"I've never...I shouldn't be...." He kissed her again and all thoughts of not touching this man flew out the window. But when he pulled back this time, she curled her hand at her side and turned away. "I'm sorry. You must think I'm a desperate school girl who's never been kissed before."

"No, I don't think that at all. I think you're a very desirable woman who I would like nothing better than to lay out on this bed and take." She looked at him then, and hated the cocky grin there. Before she could tell him to fuck off, he put his finger over her mouth and stilled the words that were ready to spew from her. "Gavin is right there. And as much as I'd like to join you in that bed, I'm pretty sure that we'd wake him up. Are you a screamer, Jasmine? I might have to rework our whole house if you are."

Images of them together popped into her head. The two of them against the wall, on the floor. She could see him taking her on the sink, in the yard against a tree. Every time he touched her she screamed, his fingers burning into her flesh like a hot brand. And Jasmine wanted more. But she couldn't, not with this man. Not with any man so long as she was being hunted.

"I am not going to have sex with you." He didn't say anything. She'd expected him, for some reason, to gloat or tell her that she was. He did neither of those things, but sat back in the chair. Jasmine had no idea why she was so pissed at him, but she was. "When I'm able to give these earrings to you, then I'm taking my son and leaving."

"Have you tried to remove them yet?" She had but didn't tell him that. He seemed to know anyway. "You can't leave them here. You can't leave me here. And if you do, then the dragon will die. And so will I. But I have a feeling that you know that already. That you've hurt yourself trying to remove them, and without success."

"He said that you'd tell me that too. But I can't stay here. You have to know that. These men, they'll stop once I've left here. I'll be safe to protect my son." Jasmine wasn't going to be pulled into any more drama. She had enough going on right now on her own. Before she could say anything more, Gavin sat up and looked at her. Then he threw his arms around her. Suddenly everything that she'd endured this far had been worth it to get back to him.

She was still holding him when she realized that Jorden

had left them. But she had a feeling that he wasn't far. Jasmine had to get out of here before Jorden hurt her. Or she hurt him. There was a good possibility that they'd hurt each other if she stayed too much longer.

CHAPTER 4

Wilburn Glass hated that things were not going his way. First that fucking bastard Gentry had taken what was his in the ring, and now the earrings had been nearly in his hands when another person had stepped in and taken them from him. He glared at the stain on the wall behind the fallen chair, and wondered who else he was going to have to kill to get things to go his way.

"The accident was supposed to have killed her. Can someone tell me what the fuck went wrong there? Or at the hospital when she should have been killed again?" The men in the room with him said nothing. Wilburn knew that they had no more answers than he did, but he wanted something. Anything to make this shit get going in his direction. "What sort of arrangements have been made to get her fingerprints, even some sort of address where she might have been taken?"

"There was nothing left in the room. And what I mean by that is, there was a fire. Hot enough to melt the bed frame to the floor and the curtains to nothing more than a stain on the floor. But oddly enough, the rest of the area was untouched."

He asked Quincy, one of his devout followers, how that was possible. "We don't know. Any video from that time is gone as well. Whatever caused the fire had been controlled; hot, but controlled all the same. And when we went to check on the cameras, there was nothing to indicate that they'd ever been running. Not before she was to arrive, nor after she supposedly disappeared. I had two men go floor to floor in every room in the event that she might have been put in a room under a different name. Nothing."

"What about outside? Surely there is something showing who came and got her, and what they might have been driving." Quincy said that they'd been searching, but there was nothing to indicate that she'd ever arrived or left. "So, we have a dead nurse, a dead cop, and nothing else to show for our time and money invested in getting this jewelry back. Do we at least have a lead on any of the other pieces? Anything?"

"No, sir. We've narrowed down where one of the smaller pieces might have been; however, it's not surfaced as yet. But we do know that it was in the estate of one of the founding fathers of Dragon." Those fucking bastards had thwarted him on more than one occasion lately. "We also know that some items, none that we've been able to trace as yet, have been mailed out, but to who or where, we're not sure of that either. We've planted people at some of the larger postal offices to see what they find, but that's turning out to be a dead end. There are just too many for us to cover all of them."

"Is there anything that you're sure of? So far all you've been able to tell me is that you know nothing of what happened to the woman when she was rammed by your men. There is no trace of her in the hospital that was set up to take care of her. The cop is dead, as is the nurse we had on the payroll. The room that she was in has no trace of her, or even that she'd been there. And you have nothing on how she got in or out of the place other than some excuses. Oh, and let us not forget that you may or may not have a lead on one of the other pieces that might or might not have belonged to one of the founders of my worst adversaries. I'm not missing anything, am I?" Wilburn laid his gun on the desk and looked pointedly at the blood stain on the wall and floor in front of him. "The last man that I sent for the jewelry only had to outbid all the other fools around him. Get my jewelry and bring it back here. But no, he was sidetracked. How the fuck did he figure that I was paying him to be sidetracked?"

Wilburn shot the man sitting next to Quincy, and smiled when they all started screaming and scrambling to get away. He aimed the gun at no one in particular, but it had the desired effect. Not only did they shut up, but they didn't move either.

"Sir, we—" He shot the man that spoke who was standing next to Quincy. Wilburn had wanted to make a point, but now he was just glad that he had their full attention.

"Now. Here is what is going to happen, now that you understand that I want answers and not excuses. You're going to find my jewelry so that I can take care of this dragon. Do you have any idea what kind of damage this monster can do to this world should he be allowed to rise up? How many of our followers he'll kill so that he can breed more of his kind? To take over the world?" No one moved, and he shot a third man in as many minutes. "Get out there and find my jewelry."

When they left him, he called Quincy back. The man looked ready to wet himself, he was so terrified. "Clean your mess up. Now." The younger man looked at the dead bodies and then nodded at him. "And when I return, there had better not be a single drop of blood on anything in this room. Do you understand me?"

Wilburn left the little offices and made his way to the larger, more appointed one in the back of his home. If these fuckers knew what he wanted the pieces for, not only would they stop trying to find them, but they might even beg him to kill them over it. The jewelry was nothing compared to what it would give him to have them all together. And once that happened, he'd be ruler. Not just of the men in his sect, but of all mankind. The dragon that would come forth would answer only to him.

When he'd been about seventeen, he'd heard his grandda talking to some idiot that worked for him. The man was a shifter, he knew that, but what he was Wilburn had no idea. Nor did he really care. His grandda had befriended the man, not for gain as Wilburn might have done, but because he'd liked the man. Wilburn had loved his tales, big ones that usually ended in bloodshed as well as loss of life for a great many people. But that night the two of them seemed to be talking about riches that didn't line their pockets, but ones that would be a sight that they'd remember long after they were dead. However the hell that was supposed to have happened. Dead was dead; you didn't see riches or have much use for them. He thought them both nuts.

"You should see them, Bill. A sight to behold. Just look at them sparkle, and they didn't even have those fancy cameras like they do now." Wilburn had looked over his grandda's shoulder at the five pieces of jewelry that someone had taken a picture of. There was no sparkle to them. No color to say what the jewels were. Nothing that made them look any different than the shit his mom wore when she dressed up to go out. "Jewels like you've never seen on each of them, and the workmanship is the best there is. Even now."

Wilburn had picked up the pictures and still saw nothing

that extraordinary, just a few pieces of what looked to him like cheap pretties that he'd given away to get himself laid. When his grandda marveled at their beauty, Wilburn asked him what he was talking about.

"Don't you see it, boy?" He shook his head and laid the picture down. Grandda had laughed and turned to the man. "I guess he ain't as pure of heart as I'd hoped he'd be. Not a bit of magic to be found in him either, I'm guessing. Bad genes, I guess."

"What do you mean, pure of heart? If you're saying that I've not been fucking around, then you'd be wrong." The slap to his face had him reaching for his gun. Even back then Wilburn would settle any and all arguments with a bullet rather than waste his time on showing them that he was right, even if he wasn't. "Don't you dare hit me again."

The second time he'd been hit, Wilburn felt his back hit the wall before he lost consciousness. His grandda was a large man with even bigger fists. When Wilburn woke, he looked at his grandda as he sat staring at him with his own gun on his lap.

"You ready to listen to me, or do I have to show you what having respect for someone means again?" Wilburn said nothing, but his grandda nodded as if he had. "You don't talk to people that are better than you like you have no respect for yourself. Talking like a whore on Friday night only cheapens you. Makes you less than a man. When you speak, if you have something to say, then people will listen to you better when you're not being vulgar and stupid."

"Yes, sir." Wilburn remembered thinking that his grandda was the stupidest man in the world if he thought that what you said made you a big man. "I don't know what the big deal is about the picture. There isn't anything there but some cheap dime store stuff."

"You can't see it because you don't want to." He tossed the black and white picture at him. "You see that ring there? Well, let me tell you what I've been told is there. A pair of dragons holding up a four carat diamond that is as pure as the ocean it was supposed to be formed from. The gold of the ring is so brilliant that it burns the eyes to look at it in the sunlight. Those earrings? They're dragons as well. Large ones that will curl around a woman's ear like a caress, the tail wrapped around the ear in a way that it looks as if he's hanging on for dear life, but would gladly fly away should the opportunity come to him."

He still saw nothing and said as much. "And it's just a picture. How do you know how blue the diamond is, or even if it is one? Have you ever seen a woman wearing it? For all you know it could be just an ugly piece of crap that might give her some kind of disease because it's unclean."

"You go on thinking that, son. You just go on thinking that they're worthless. But mark my words, when those pieces are all together again, and they will be someday, a great dragon will come forth, and he will bring riches to anyone who owns them." That got his attention. Riches, something that Wilburn felt you could never have enough of, was something he understood better than anything else. And still did to this day, as a matter of fact. "The family that owned them will rise up from the earth and be the greatest dragons ever seen."

"Real dragons?" Wilburn had asked his grandfather, who told him yes, real dragons. "You're telling me that the people that have this crappy jewelry are a bunch of dragons."

"No, they lost it long ago. No one knows why as yet; someday that might come out as well, but they lost their inheritance, and in doing so, their ability to become what they are. Their true selves. Dragons." Wilburn wanted to laugh at the old man, but didn't. He would get hit again, and he hated being in pain. "You'll see. Might not be now, but I'm betting sometime these pieces are going to start showing up and that family, whoever they are, is gonna have it all."

Wilburn hadn't taken his grandda seriously…not until years later, when he'd come across an article in a local paper about myths and legends. He might not have bothered with reading it, but the same picture his grandda had shown him was among the many that had been placed in the article. The story, much like his grandda had told him, had been there, even telling that each of the pieces would be worth millions all on their own. Together? Well, the article had hinted that the amount was incomprehensible. Wilburn could comprehend a huge number, and seeing that article had gotten him to look for the pieces. It had cost him a small fortune for the little information that he could gather, but it all seemed to be real.

But getting men to help him, to take him seriously, had been harder than finding information about the jewelry. So, one night when he'd been watching television with his girlfriend while his wife was out of town, he watched this program on cults and how even the dumbest people had to have something to believe in enough to do the work. And to think he almost didn't watch it over having his dick blown. Life was funny like that, he supposed.

After doing some research on gathering a fold, he found that they didn't much care to have whatever you wanted them to believe in to be factual, or even to be for a good thing. In fact, he'd found that more start up cults that dealt with killing something or destroying it survived the first few years than did those that were for a good cause. So Death to all Dragons came to be. He'd found out recently that someone had even come up with a logo for the group, and some had even gotten to wearing the saying, in different languages, on their bodies. He'd hit upon a gold mine when he started charging dues to be a member of his exclusive club. Now all he needed was the fucking jewelry to make it all come together.

~~~

"Thank you." Maxwell and his wife, Abby, had been waiting on her hand and foot since she'd gotten out of bed an hour ago. When she told them that she only wanted to sit for a little while, perhaps go outside, they both had helped her down the stairs and out onto the lovely deck that seemed to be as big as the flipping house. And the view was spectacular. She sipped the glass of tea that had been set beside her. She didn't want to get used to this, but it sure did make her feel good to know that someone cared for her, even if they were getting paid to do so.

Gavin and Jorden had gone into town early this morning. She wasn't sure she wanted to let him go, she'd only just gotten back to him, but he looked so sad when she questioned him about it.

"We're looking for venues for this charity thing that is going to happen in a couple of months. There will be dinner served, so there needs to be a kitchen, I guess. Aisha, Mrs. McCade, and the other Mrs. McCade, Emma, they're raising money for different organizations to help with school supplies and help with heating bills in the winter months, Jorden told me. I guess they're having this dinner thing where people come and eat then go home. You should come with us. Get out of the house for a bit." She wanted to, but they all knew that it was dangerous for her to be venturing out just yet. There were people looking for her. So when he left her, she decided that she'd not get any better just lying about, and had asked to sit outside. Jasmine thought that while the view was different, it was no less boring to sit here.

When a big man came out of the woods behind the house, she yelled for Maxwell.

"That would be Jorden's brother, Vance." She nodded as Vance made his way to where she was. "I'm afraid that of all the McCade men, I know the least about him. I don't think his family knows much either, my lady."

When Vance asked to have a seat on the deck with her, she nodded. When he sat in one of the larger chairs, she heard it groan. Vance wasn't just tall, but big everywhere, like he worked out using cars as weights. He tilted back his worn dirty hat, a black Stetson, and looked at her. After a few minutes, he finally spoke to her.

"You know that you're being looked for, don't you?" She told him that she did. "I figured you did. What I'm afraid that you might not know is that they're closing in on you and that boy of yours. I ran into a couple of them in town."

"Ran into them or ran over them?" He just smiled. Jasmine had been kidding, but his look told her that she didn't want to know the real answer. "They want these earrings. I've tried to get them off, but they're stuck there. I think I might need to have them removed by a surgeon or something."

"They're not coming off unless you want to get rid of those pretty ears too. They're a part of you. Just as much as your son and Jorden now, I guess." Again she wasn't sure if he was kidding or not, but didn't ask. When he leaned back on the chair, she saw the gun. Jasmine had an idea that his gun was as much a part of him as her earrings were to her. "Are you afraid of me?"

"Honestly? I don't know. You're quiet and very observant, but I think that in your mind lurks something that I don't want to know about." He nodded but said nothing. "I don't think you showed your gun to scare me, more…I think you just didn't think about it being there until I saw it. You're not a terrible person, but I think you feel you've done some pretty terrible things. I have no idea why I think that, but I do."

"I'm sorry about the gun. And you're right, I don't think of it unless I need to use it. It's there because I have needed it. Ever since I've been back from places better left unnamed." She nodded and looked at the tree line when he did. "The man that's after you, he doesn't care for the dragon, even though he wants others to think he does. He wants the riches that come with owning the dragon. Do you know the legend, Jasmine?"

"Some of it. I'm not sure how much of what I've been told is true, but I've heard it. You're one too." He nodded. "I don't know a lot of history about this whole thing, as I said. I know what Emma told me, and the dragon. But I don't think he knows that much either. He seems to be as lost as anyone about what he can do, and what is coming with each piece. And what happens once they're all here."

Vance stood up and handed her a sheet of paper. It was a picture of all the pieces, she'd bet. "Do you see them as they are in the photo, or do you see them at their best?" She asked him what he meant. "What do you see when you look at the brooch there in the middle? Just tell me what you see and I'll tell you what I know."

"All right." Jasmine picked up the picture off her lap. "I see a dragon on an oval piece of onyx, I think. His body is blue, small stones that I think are sapphires seem to merge together into a larger piece that makes him glitter and glow. He has emeralds for eyes and his wings…. His wings look like they're made of some kind of opal; blue opal, I think. The pendant is made of gold, brilliantly polished so that it's almost painful to look at."

"The picture, to most people — humans — is in black and white. Nor do they see them as you and the rest of us do. They see, as they're meant to, just a bunch of cheap looking jewelry that they don't understand the fuss over. Those that cannot see the pieces for what they are have no magic in them. And being a dragon, or any shifter, is magic." She said that she had never seen a shifter or magic until coming here. "Not true. You know several shifters where you lived. I've talked to a few of them. Mr. Brown, the butcher, he's a cat. The woman who would ring you out at the grocery store was a wolf. Those animals there, the ones that you can see along the tree line, they're shifters as well. And once you are comfortable with them, they'll come and introduce themselves to you." Jasmine looked at the three wolves that were staring at her like they knew she was thinking about them.

"What does this have to do with the picture?" Vance laid it on his lap and closed his eyes. Jasmine wondered if he was going to answer her, and decided that while she really wanted to know, she wasn't good at playing games.

"When they come for you, you'll have to do just what we tell you to do or you'll be killed." The calmness in his voice, the way he said it as if he were talking about the coming rain, chilled her to her very core. "There are two men, even as we sit here, that are finding clues as to where you are and what you're doing. At first I thought them working together, gathering what they could to combine their efforts to come for you. But they're not. One is coming soon, the other is biding his time. Waiting for the other man to make a mistake. Or to get a piece of the jewelry that he already thinks of as his."

"They mean to kill whoever has a piece of it, like Emma and myself do, or take it before someone else can put a claim on it. And the picture? What does it have to do with me?" Vance told her everything. "Can you just stop talking to me like we're on some game show and simply tell me what you're trying hard not to say? In the event that you didn't notice, these men hurt me and mine. I want them gone from my life as much as you guys do."

He laughed, but she wasn't sure that it made her feel any better. "The men that are looking for the other pieces, they have been instructed to do whatever is necessary to get them. Even if the owner, as you are with the earrings, happens to be wearing them. When they find what he wants they're to cut the pieces from the woman, using any and all means possible, then kill her if she's not already dead. Should they find you, they won't bother with your ears, as I have said… they'll simply cut your head off, ship it to him, and he'll store it away, head and all, until all the pieces come to him." She asked him how he knew this. He just handed her the picture again. This time she saw the fingerprint. It was small and barely noticeable until he pointed it out to her. The one that seemed to be smeared in blood. "The person that owned the picture was the grandfather to the man who now comes for you. He will kill, indiscriminately, until he gets what he wants. But what he doesn't know, and he'll find out, is that I won't hesitate to keep you and the other women that come here safe. We will all do whatever is necessary to do so. But you must promise me that when I tell you to do something, whatever it might be, you must do it. It will save your life."

"Will they hurt Gavin?" He only looked at her. "Then I have to ask you to make me a promise. I will do whatever you need, whenever you need it, but you have to keep him safe. No matter what, Gavin is all I have in this world, and I won't be able to do anything if I don't know that he's safe."

"If I promise you that he is safe, will you trust me?" Trust. A word that she wasn't sure about. "None of us will never lie to you. Never harm you, and I will protect you both, and my entire family, with my life. If I promise you that he is taken care of, will you trust me that I'm not telling you a falsehood?"

"Yes." It was a huge step for her, to trust this stranger. When he stood up, she felt like she needed to hug him, to tell him that whatever happened to him—because she knew something had—it would be all right. But she'd not lie to him either. "Jorden thinks he's my mate. He said that when I leave here, he will die with the dragon."

"If you leave here before this is finished, I cannot protect you. And in this fight, I'm your only hope." That scared her to death. "Stay or leave, it's up to you, but should you do so, then know that you both will die, and it won't be an easy one for either of you." With that, Vance walked off the deck and back into the woods, with the wolves behind him.

Jasmine was still sitting on the deck, everything around her faded in the back of her mind, when Jorden said her name. She wasn't sure that being stuck here was the right word, but she couldn't leave. Because for every scenario she thought of that they could do to her and Gavin, she was sure there were a hundred more things she didn't let her mind dwell on. They were here until things were taken care of. Whatever that meant.

"Maxwell said that Vance came to see you." She nodded. "Are you all right? I know that he won't hurt you, but he's a little intense and can be a little abrupt. Few know that he's still working for the government, and that they can and do call for him when things are bad. But he's a wonderful man and would do anything for anyone. But as I said, he can be a little scary, even to us."

"He said he'd protect us, but the only way that he could do that is if we stayed here." Jorden said nothing but watched her. "I was married once. I know that you are aware of that and the circumstances surrounding it. I don't trust easily, if at all, and my son is my entire world. What I'm trying to say is, I don't know what to do about you and your family, or what it is that you want from us."

"What is it you think we want for you to do?" She told him she had no idea. "All right, that's fair enough. But can I tell you what I want? What I'd like to see happen between us?"

"You want to fuck me." He shook his head. "Come on, you're not going to sit there and tell me you don't want to have sex with me. I might be a little rusty when it comes to sex, but I know when someone wants me."

"I do want you. Badly as a matter of fact. All I can think about is laying you out on my bed and feasting on every single part of you. Then when I've had my tongue on every single part of you, I want to start over. I want to bury my cock deep into you, fill you with all that I am, and have you scream out my name while I do so." Jasmine shifted on her seat when he touched his fingers to her cheek. "No, Jasmine, I don't want to merely fuck you, I want to make love to you. Make love with you. Bring your body to peak with all that I am, not because you're a woman, but because I want you to belong to me."

Tears filled her eyes at his soft words. They were kind and loving. She was sure that he meant them too, that he'd not been just telling her things that he thought she wanted to hear. Kris had done that all the time, and she'd hated it.

"I don't know how to be what you need." He asked her what it was she thought he might need. "I don't know. I'm not sure. When I was married the first time, even before we were married a full two days, he told me that I wasn't what he wanted in a bed partner. And that he'd never loved me, only saw me as a means to get what he wanted from his mom. He cared for me, but he'd never love me, he told me. And if I hadn't sort of forced his hand that first night we were together, I'm pretty sure that he wouldn't have ever had sex with me."

"From all accounts of Kris that we were able to find, he wasn't a very good man. I mean, he might have been had his mom not messed with his life, but he should have taken better care with you and Gavin. Money, it seems, was more important to him than simply seeing that he had responsibilities that had nothing to do with his sexual preferences." She nodded and looked away. "Jasmine, Gavin will never feel like he's not important to me. I'll provide for you and him like he's my own child. And any we might have later, if you wish, they will only know him as Gavin, their big brother. I want him to carry my name, be a McCade, not because I've married his mom — and that is what I want more than anything — but because I love you and him enough to make sure the world knows it."

"I don't know what I want or need right now other than to be safe. And Gavin will need to know that you're not just saying pretty words to get his mom in the sack. He has to trust you more than I do right now." He said he understood that. "Can you? Can you know what it's like to not have any idea if the next person that comes around the corner is going to try and kill you? That every time Gavin isn't in your sight, you wonder if he's safe?"

"Yes." She stared at him. "Gavin might not be of my body, but he's like a son to me already, and will be if you consent to it. I know this is too soon, that you're still trying to get your feet under you, but I'm in love with you."

"No, that's not possible. You just.... It's just the need to have sex, that's all. You're a man that needs to have sex, and that's all you're feeling right now." He stood up but didn't move. She was worried that she might have hurt him in some way. "I'm sorry, Jorden, I really am, but I'm slightly overwhelmed right now and I don't know what way is up."

"I want to take you to my bed and make love to you for hours. When I see you lying in my bed, it's all I can do not to join you. I haven't, do you know why?" She said that she didn't. "Because I want you to trust that what I say to you is truth. That when I tell you that I want you, it's not because I'm some horny kid, but because I want to make love to you, cherish every part of you. Do I want to simply bend you over this railing and fuck you hard? Hell yeah, I do. But because I love you, not because you're here and wearing a part of me you brought to life."

"Brought to life?"

Jorden nodded to her and stepped off the deck. Before she could ask him where he was going, he was gone. And in his place was the most beautiful creature she'd ever seen. His dragon was even more amazing than the man had been.

CHAPTER 5

Jorden wasn't sure who was more surprised by his shift, her or him. He'd known that he'd be able to shift, in theory, but not how easy it was. And when he spread out his wings behind him, she stood up despite her being hurt. Her fingers danced over his flesh, making him tingle within the dragon. And when he moaned, he felt the dragon smile, as if he wasn't wholly him but someone else.

"Can you fly?" He had no idea, but looked up to the sky when she did. "Try it. Dragon said that my earrings would bring you your wings. Show me, Jorden. I want to see you in the sky so badly I can almost taste the excitement of it."

You can fly, my lord. As can Lord Kenton. Just think of lifting up and you should be able to do it. He asked him what he meant by should be able to do it. *I have not flown in many, many generations, sadly. I have spent so many years apart because of the magic that I can no longer remember what it feels like to be in the air. Should you do this now, as the lady wishes, you'll not only please her but me as well.*

I'm sorry. Dragon told him it was all right, but he should please his mate and fly with her. *Not until I know what I'm doing. What if I drop her? Or I fall from the sky?*

You will not. But Jorden wanted to wait, and when Jasmine told him again to fly for her, he thought of soaring upward. When he lifted from the ground with only a little effort, he felt wonderful. And his dragon did as well...his joy ran over him as Jasmine's fingers had. *You should tell her. Let her know what you are thinking. You have a connection now. All of those that have come to be with their mates, we can speak this way.*

I love you. He heard Jasmine giggle and he smiled. Something so small as a laugh made him feel as if he'd conquered the world. *You should take pictures of me. I haven't any idea what I look like.*

"You're beautiful. I mean, simply the most beautiful creature I've ever seen. Your wings are blue, but like the sky blue, not the ocean. And when you're spread out the way you are now, I can't see them...they're a perfect match for what's around you." He landed on the ground in front of the deck, bowing before her and Gavin, who had come to join them. "He wants to ride with you. Take him up, please, but be careful."

Reaching for him, it never occurred to him to think it might be a bad idea but took Gavin up in the air. The boy's laughter, his excitement, was well worth the small fear he'd had. And when he turned in the sky, letting Gavin see what he wanted, Jorden thought he could die a happy man right now when Gavin told him he was the best person in the world.

Jorden held him tightly, not painfully, but he wasn't going to drop him. And when Gavin's laughter touched his ears again, Jorden laughed with him. Never would he have thought that he'd be flying, much less with his son. Landing on the grass, he reached for Jasmine this time. And when she backed away, he knew it wasn't from fear of him but of the unknown. When he took a step toward her again, she came to him willingly and he wrapped her into his arms. They were in the sky in seconds.

They weren't high, not as high as he'd been the first time he'd gone up…he knew that she was afraid of him dropping her. He showed her what he had shown Gavin. The top of their home. And Kenton's. The town that they had been in only hours ago. He pointed out landmarks that he could see, and showed her the places where their land touched his family's.

Taking her to one of the hills behind their home, he landed on his feet and turned her in his arms as he shifted to himself. Taking her mouth with his own, he felt her respond to him like she had before, needy and hungry for him. He lifted his head just enough to speak to her. He nibbled on her between thoughts.

"There is no bed here, but I need to be inside of you." She nodded, pulling at his clothing. "Christ, all I can think about is taking you right here, on the ground."

"Then less talking and more getting naked." He laughed when she did. "I think it was the excitement of seeing you like that. A dragon. You have any idea how…? You brought him to life, made me believe that this might be worth it. Hurry, Jorden. I need you."

"I see, you want me for the dragon and not for my lovely body." Jorden pretended to pout when he dropped to his knees in front of her. "I'm going to enjoy this more than you can imagine."

Burying his mouth over her pussy, he could smell her need even through her panties. He pulled them down a little at a time, tasting her skin as he exposed it. When they were down around her knees, he pulled her to him again and licked her hard nubbin that seemed to be begging him to bite. Taking

71

her into his mouth, Jorden moaned at the taste of her.

She flooded his mouth with her cream. It was hot, spicy, and thick. Jorden lifted her leg up to get more of her, but all it did was tease him more. He wanted all of her, not just the little he could get with her standing up. Begging her to lie down, he helped her strip out of her shirt and bra. Then when she was on the ground before him, Jorden stood up and took off his own clothing. Christ, he hurt, he needed her so badly.

When he pulled his shirt off and dropped it atop her things, she sat up and rubbed her cheek over his cock. He could have come right then, just let his cum fill his boxers rather than his mate. And if she kept it up, which it looked as if she might, he would. But he needed to be deep inside of her and he backed from her. Jorden took off the last of his clothing. When she told him to stand still, he wasn't sure what she needed until she reached for his cock, wrapping her hand around him.

"You're very hard." He nodded and moaned when she kissed the tip of his cock. "Every time I hear the shower running or find a damp towel in the bathroom, all I can think about is seeing you like this. Naked and hard. And when I take the towel that you used to my nose, I think of it rubbing over your body, how hard it must be when you scrub yourself. Christ, it's all I can do not to hunt you down and beg you to take me again and again."

Jasmine ran her tongue over the tip of his cock, then circled his crown. When she sucked him into her mouth for the briefest of seconds, he felt his balls tighten up. And then when she let him go, he grabbed the tree next to him and held on, knowing that he was that close to falling on his ass.

"I've had to relieve myself every time I'm alone. Just thinking of you touching me, it hurts." She licked him from tip to root, pausing long enough to take his balls into her mouth one at a time. "I'm so close, Jasmine. And unless you want me to come all over you like this, let me eat you."

She laid back, her body beautiful against the dark grass, her hair spread out under her head. He looked at her, really looked, and told her how incredibly gorgeous she was.

"I'm not." He got down on his knees again and she shivered. "You're going to bring me over to your dark side, aren't you? I have to tell you; I've never had oral sex before. So while I know theoretically what is going to happen, I'm a little afraid of disappointing you."

"What a shame. But then, I'm very happy to introduce you to something so wonderful that you're never going to want me to stop." She giggled again. "Christ, I could go every day and be happy just to hear you laugh."

Kissing her inner thigh, Jorden wondered how he should start. Slowly, his mind told him, but his body said go for it. Spreading her tender lips open, he could see how wet she was, how hard her little clit was. Taking it into his mouth, he bit down hard enough to bring her but not taste her blood. He would do that some other time, he thought. And when she screamed again as he sucked her into his mouth, Jorden slid his fingers into her to see if he could make her come at least a dozen or more times before he took her. If he didn't die first.

She rode his mouth, then his fingers. Every time she begged him to stop, to let her rest, he would begin again, bringing her harder, faster than before. Jasmine was his, and he was going to make sure that she enjoyed this as much as he did, even if it killed him. When she pulled his head up by jerking his hair, he was breathing hard, his body hurting to take her.

"I need you to stop." He shook his head. "Yes. You've made your point. You enjoy oral sex and so do I, but I'm exhausted. I never knew a body could come that many times."

73

"Oh, but that was only the appetizer. Now I'm going to have you as my main course, as well as dessert, before I can declare myself filled." She was shaking her head even as she reached for him. Jorden tasted her navel as he made his way up her body. Nipped at her hip. When he licked a path up her ribs, he knew she was close again; her hips were rising up to meet his and he teased her a little with his cock. "When I fill you, I will come quickly, I'm sorry to say."

"I need you." He slid the thick crown of his cock into her and paused. "More. Please, I need more. Jorden, fill me please?"

He slammed forward even as he took her mouth. He tasted her climax, felt her scream all the way down his back. When she dug her nails into his skin, drawing blood that he felt run down his spine, Jorden fucked her hard, pounding her as hard as he could, filling not just her pussy with himself but everywhere he could touch her. And when he felt his body ready to release, he threw back his head and cried out as he emptied. Every part of his body, every cell inside of him, exploded as he released deep within his mate.

Even as the thought that he was done entered his mind, his body spent, he felt himself fill again, and his cock thicken. And when his balls ached again, he leaned into her throat and licked her pulse there. As soon as she screamed she was coming, he bit down and came with her, his mouth filled with her blood even as his body filled her with his cum.

Bringing her once more, hearing her beg him to please let her rest, Jorden knew that she was his. Marking her with his cum and taking her blood, he also knew that no one would hurt her so long as he was alive if he could help it. And he'd love her with his dying breath.

Dropping down, his body rolling at the last second to pull

hers onto his, he held her. When his heart wasn't feeling like he'd run a race and had given it his all, he might be able to tell her again how much he loved her. But for now, he could barely move. Closing his eyes, Jorden smiled. He had his mate.

Waking to the sound of some of the forest animals coming back out into the area, he laid still while he watched a pair of wolves leap and run around as if they had not a care in the world. He supposed so long as they stayed here, where he could protect them, they didn't. When Jasmine lifted her head up and looked down at him, he brushed the tears away and asked her what was wrong.

"I don't know. Nothing and everything. I never wanted this, another man in my life." He nodded, trying his best not to be wounded by her words. "I mean, you're a wonderful man and probably could have done better than me, but I never wanted to fall in love with you."

"I love you as well." She nodded and laid her head back down. He smacked her on the ass hard, and when she lifted her head up again, he kissed her. "I couldn't have done any better than you. As far as I'm concerned, you're perfect. And why shouldn't you be? I'm perfect as well."

She laughed with him, but he could tell she was still thinking about them being together. But instead of trying to reassure her again, which he wasn't sure she'd believe, Jorden told her about his art and the exhibit that was coming up.

"When I was a kid growing up knowing that I wanted to work in art, I wasn't sure what I wanted to work with. Paint, clay. I even played around with pen and inks for a time. But something about the way colors flow together in painting makes me love it the best. When I'm working, which hasn't been very much since you've been around, I get excited to see a blank canvas, the colors on my pallet there just waiting to be mixed together and put to the material." She looked at him. "Like you. When I first saw you, I honestly was terrified of you. Not you really, but what you would become now. As my mate."

"You mean what you could change me into?" He said no, that wasn't it at all. He loved her just the way she was. "Then I don't understand. Why did I frighten you?"

"I was afraid that you'd change from the picture that Gavin had painted in my head of you." He knew that he wasn't explaining it well. "Gavin told me all these stories about you. How you took on that proctor at the college. When you had a man trying to date you and he had a wife and children. He gave me a side of you that made me see you in this way that I bet few see you in. A protective mother. A warrior for the underdog. Someone that cries at sappy commercials and gets excited about a box of junk that no one else wanted that you only paid a buck for. He told me of the times he would see you sitting at your desk when you thought him in bed, writing descriptions for your pieces to flip, and the two of you laughing at the stories you made up for him about the people you'd encounter. The woman that he showed me, the woman that you are, was the person I fell in love with long before you came to me. And you are just that woman, all of the things I said and more."

"Oh Jorden, what a way with words you have." He kissed her then, giving her a small taste of what he felt for her. And when he looked up at her when she lifted her head, Jorden fell more in love with her than he'd been before. He truly did love his mate.

~~~

Gavin was sitting in the living room when Jasmine came into the house. Maxwell told her that he'd been in there a little while, but he had told him that he was thinking. Gavin did that better than most, and when he came to her about it, he had whatever plan or scheme completely worked out in his head before he opened his mouth.

"I would like to go to college." She nodded and sat down when Gavin spoke. "I'm not sure what I want to be, there are so many things that I love doing, but I do want to finish up my education and go to college. One that will help me. If you don't mind."

"No. You know that you and I are on the same page about your education. Whatever you want to do, you know that I'm going to support you in any way I can. Is this because you want to go abroad? I have the funds for that now, if that's what you're thinking. But before you answer that, I have a question or two for you." He told her that he figured as much. "Good. Are you doing this because you don't want to be a part of the family, or do you really want to go? And before you answer that one, I know that you think we're going to discard you like yesterday's empty boxes."

"Did Jorden tell you that?" She grinned at him and told him Gavin just had. "Okay, tricky Mom, but I'm right and I think you know that too. You have Jorden now, and while I really like him, even love him a lot, I know that I can never be his son, and when you have some of his kids, I'm not going to fit in."

"Really? And how do you figure that? You mean because you aren't a McCade? I have news for you, buddy. He's already asked me if he can adopt you and give you his name." That perked him up, but Gavin was ever cautious, just as she was. "What would you think of having a little brother or sister? We've not talked about it, Jorden and I, but I'd never do anything like that, have more family, unless it was what we all wanted. I can't do that to us."

"He loves you." Jasmine told Gavin that she loved him as well. "I like him, probably even love him if you want to know the truth. He's a nice person and his family is awesome. He doesn't talk to me like I'm some kid he wants to impress, and when he doesn't know something or even when he knows a lot more than me, he doesn't dance on my head and call me names."

"No, he'd never do what your father did to you, and I'm glad that you recognize that in him. Aisha said she wanted you to call her Grandma. You'd be her first, she told me." The pain of her own grannie, laying in a grave unmarked as yet, hurt her. "You don't have to, but I think Dalton said you call him Uncle once in a while."

All the McCade men had told her what a great kid he was. How polite he was, and helpful. They'd told her what a great job she'd done raising a good man, and had asked her, each of them, if she would let him call them Uncle. She told them it was up to Gavin.

"Vance is really great; he's sort of scary quiet, but I like him. Lewis is funny, and can make almost anything that you want to eat. Even if he has to make things up, he does a great job at it. He and Aunt Emma have these cook-off things, did you know that? She'll make something for him to try, and he has to guess what's in it and how much of each ingredient. The fresh herbs that she has in her garden are throwing him off. But now he wants me to help him put an herb garden in too." Jasmine didn't cook, hated it even, and Gavin knew it. "Abby cooks for us here. I told her that you could order all kinds of food to be brought to us, but you didn't like to clean up or make it."

Jasmine pinched him. "That wasn't nice." He laughed and

she did as well. "Well, okay, my next question for you. And this is a biggie, all right? Are you so ready to give all of this family up so soon after we got them? I'm thinking you don't want to, but are unsure of them. I am too, if you want the truth, but I think of all the people we've known in our life, these guys are the real deal."

He looked at her then, his face sad and his eyes looking older than her. She loved this boy, more than she did anything in the world, and told him that every day. When he laid his head on her breast, just holding her, she ran her fingers through his hair as she'd done when he was a baby.

"I'm afraid." She said she was as well. "We only had each other for so long, and then one morning, I woke up and we were on a plane, and then Grannie died. I don't think I could do that again, Mom...lose someone that I love like that. Nor do I want to ever leave you behind because it was safer for me."

"I don't want you hurt, Gavin. You understand why I did that." He said that he did, but it didn't make it any less painful. "I won't send you away again unless it's life or death. I promise you. There is little to nothing I can do about death, honey, but know that I'm going to do everything in my power to keep living for you."

Jorden joined them a few minutes later. He didn't crowd onto the couch where they were, but sat in the big chair beside them. She loved him for that. Giving her and Gavin time to be with each other. When popcorn and drinks were brought in to them, he joined them then, sitting on the floor while they found something to watch on the big screen television.

"Why do you have such a monster of a house, Jorden?" He laughed at Gavin's question, and leaned back as the commercial was muted. "I mean, this is an awesome house—

Mom could sell these things in here for a lot of cash—but it's huge. Even for you."

"I bought it off of Emma for an unbelievably great price. This was her father's home. She told me that she could never live here—they were estranged, you see—but she wanted someone to move in and love it for her. Make it into a home, not a house." Gavin nodded as if he understood, then shook his head. "Not a good enough reason?"

"No. There's more, I think. You seem like a polished new stuff sort of person, not old dusty like my mom." She pinched him again, this time harder, then told him he was right. "You know what I mean…you like the old things. I do too, but I don't think any of these things are what you'd buy for yourself. I mean, even keep around if you didn't want to. Right?"

"You're right. I wouldn't have bought this for myself. But I love it. And while I do miss a few modern things, like a filing cabinet that fits legal papers, a phone that is younger than me, I do love the way these things are built, the quality that went into making each piece. I do have plans of modernizing some of the things here. We need better lines coming in for Internet. Now that you're here, you can help me get that fixed up. I also want to fix up the pool. It's a nice one, but I'd very much like to have a heated one to use year round, wouldn't you?" He looked around when she did. "Perhaps the fates knew that I'd find me an old dusty wife and son, and decided that I'd be perfect here."

"That's a sappy answer. And the next person that calls me old and dusty is going to eat whatever I cook tomorrow night for dinner." Gavin promised her he'd never call her that again, and rolled his eyes at them when Jasmine kissed Jorden.

"You can keep your old and dusty, Dad, but I want a room that I can decorate on my own. If you don't mind." He stood up then. "I would also like to work on getting a computer for my room. I'll work it off if it costs too much."

When he was gone, just getting up and leaving them there, Jasmine looked at Jorden. He looked like someone had punched him in the head and was still trying to recover from it. When she said his name for the second time, he finally looked at her.

"He called me Dad." She nodded. "I mean, just said it like he's done it his whole life. *Dad, I want a room of my own.* I don't think I've heard a more beautiful sentence than that. Except for when you say you love me."

"The next thing you know, he's going to be asking you to borrow your car keys and telling you that he's knocked some girl up and needs you to help him." Jorden grinned. "I was kidding. He'd better never knock some girl up or I'll kill him."

"You need a car." She asked him where that came from. "I just realized it. You need a car, and Gavin does need a new room. Whatever he wants. We'll have to wait a bit to actually go to some stores, I think, but we can have him start looking online for what he wants. And a computer first and foremost. He told me the other day that he is a little behind on taking some classes."

"His being behind might mean that he's only four lessons ahead, not ten. And you're not going to spoil him because he called you Dad, are you?" He shook his head, but told her verbally that he was planning on it. "The two of you are going to be the death of me, you know that, don't you?"

"Nope, we're going to make things fun. Can you sell the things in his room? Whatever he doesn't want? *Wait.*" He stood up suddenly and started pacing. "There is an old building in town. I got it with the studio. Change it into a shop. Fill it with antiques that you find and deals that you buy in boxes of junk.

It would be perfect for you. And you'd be close enough to me that when the urge hit you, you could come on over and come with me."

"Just like that, you want me to open a junk antique store. How do you know if I could even make a go at it? I might not know anything about antiques." He just cocked a brow at her. "You're nuts, you know that, right? Who would buy things in a shop that I run?"

"I can think of a lot of people off the top of my head. Mrs. Dunlap…I don't remember what she got off of you, something that smashed your hand, but she would. And Mr. Rosen. You've not met him, but he is opening this little bed and breakfast that has older things in it. I bet he could use a few pieces. Then there is the restaurant that Lewis wants to open someday. You could help him get deals on things like tables and chairs and stuff like that."

"Slow down a bit there. In the event that you've forgotten, I have a murderer after me." He pulled her from the couch and kissed her. "So we're not worried about him?"

"Oh we are, but we can't let him rule our lives. If he wants to come for you, let him. I think we can take the bastard." He kissed her again. "Also, we're getting married. How about next weekend? I think Emma can have a cake ready for us, and Gavin can give you away. I love it."

She was still standing there ten minutes after he left her, saying something about plans and an open bar. When Abby came in to ask her if she needed anything else, a thousand things popped into her head. But she only shook her head. Jorden McCade had just asked her…no, he'd told her she was going to marry him. And Jasmine was thrilled to death.

82

CHAPTER 6

Jorden was just applying the gesso to the canvas when he looked up. The man sitting in his chair startled not only him, but also his dragon. As he was getting ready to call the police, dragon told him to wait.

"May I help you?" The man didn't speak but looked around the room. "I'm sorry. How did you get in here?"

"I picked the lock. You need more security in here. Your home is much better, but it's the pack that roams around that is going to save you." Jorden reached for Dalton. "I don't think you want to call anyone else in if that is in fact what you're doing. I would hate to have someone get hurt over nothing. My men have instructions not to let us be disturbed."

I think I might need you here. And some men. This man claims to have some men here that would hurt anyone that came to help me. Dalton laughed. *He said he picked the lock of this building and that I need more security.*

I told you that the other day. That your stupid flimsy lock wasn't going to keep a ten-year-old out. But I'm on my way. And so you know, these people could not be more obvious. There are three big black SUVs right outside your building that nearly scream, 'come and see what I'm up to.' Dalton laughed again. *Vance is with me, so be prepared for some blood.*

"Did you hear me, young man? You don't need to call anyone in here. I only want to talk to you about a deal I think we can strike up. And if you call people in, I might not be ready to talk."

Jorden just shook his head as he sat on the corner of his work table. "Well, that's too fucking bad. I don't know who you are, nor do I think I want to." The man reached into his suit pocket, but paused when Gavin seemed to come out of nowhere and put the gun to his head. Jorden wasn't sure if he was glad or terrified to see the young man do that for them. "Secure or not, you should do better at figuring shit out before you invade someone's space."

"Very good. I have to admit, I didn't think of the boy." The man put his hands out but didn't move. Gavin glanced at him, and Jorden walked to him and took the gun. Gavin faded back into the room he'd been in without a word. "It was the boy, wasn't it? I have been keeping tabs on all of you over the last few days. He's been with you a great deal. I should have expected he'd continue to be so. Where is his mom? She's the one that they'd be hunting for."

"I have no idea what you're talking about. However, now that we've established that I'm not nearly as stupid as you thought and that my son is here a lot, who are you and what are you doing here?" The man asked if he could reach into his pocket. "If it's a gun, you'll never get it out."

"No. It's a picture. One that I'm sure you've seen before." Jorden told him to use his left hand and the man nodded. When he had it out and handed it to him, Jorden heard a commotion down in the lower level and wondered if Dalton was all right.

"That is the jewelry that your family needs, right? I'm right, aren't I?"

While he is no threat to you at the moment, continue as you have been but do not trust him. I know not what he is about, but I know that he means you no harm. At the moment. Jorden asked the dragon how the man knew about Jasmine. *I think he will explain. If not, I will find the information for you. I do not think, however, that he will be happy with me in his mind.*

Jorden glanced at the picture but said nothing. It did look like the ring that Emma wore, as well as the earrings that Jasmine now had on, but there was something decidedly off about it. Putting the picture down on the table next to him, he waited for the man to speak. But when the doors opened behind him and there stood not just Dalton, but Vance as well, Jorden had to admit, he did feel better.

"This man just showed up with some goons down there. Did they give you any trouble?" Vance only laughed and Dalton said he thought he might have broken a nail. "I'm guessing not then."

Vance sat next to him and picked up the picture, saying nothing. Dalton went to the room where Gavin was and returned with him. When Vance put the photo back down, he looked at the man. Whatever was going on, his brother knew more than Jorden did. When he turned to him, Jorden was slightly afraid. Not of his brother but of what he might know.

"This is an artist's rendition of what the pieces look like. They might have gotten some vague information about what they might look like, the colors the dragon might be wearing. Someone, not sure who, has made hard copies of them and then took this picture, trying to pawn it off as the real jewelry that he has seen. Whoever it is, and I'm working on that, doesn't have the ability to see the pieces; nor, in this case, do they have any clue where they are. The green of the wings, it's nothing like the green of the actual piece, if I remember correctly. And if you look hard enough, you can see small differences in the pieces that were made on spec." The wings weren't green on the ring at all, but blue, and Vance knew that as well as Jorden did. Vance looked at the man as he continued. "Not very nice of you to go around showing off this fake, Richard. I thought we talked about this."

"Wilburn is coming here, I told you that. When he gets here, he's not going to be nice about getting information that he wants. And so you know, I just broke in here without much in the way of effort." Vance said nothing, but he did take the gun from him. Jorden wasn't surprised when he laid it on the table by the picture. "You're not going to hurt me again, are you, Vance? I told you that I'd tell you the truth from now on. I just wanted to see if your brother here would sell me the pieces that he has."

The man, Richard, was human, and while Vance wasn't, Jorden was pretty sure that he could kill the man without much effort even if he had been human too. When Vance stood up, Richard cringed. Jorden was pretty sure that Vance had no idea how much the little man was afraid of him.

"You said that you'd call me in when you knew what was going on. I've not heard anything from you." Vance looked at Jorden, then back at Richard as the man continued. "I'm your partner. You and I have a deal, don't we?"

"Richard here is the brother to the man who started the group known as the Death to all Dragons clan. They really weren't much, just a bunch of men that gathered together once in a while and talked about taking down a dragon. Then they found out about us and the jewelry, and his brother, Wilburn, got it in his head that he would benefit more from the pieces than we would. But as far as I know, he hasn't been all that successful in keeping any of it. Wilburn Glass is his name. His group is well-funded…stupid, but well-funded, and they want to get the pieces before they all come together." Jorden had about a million questions run through his mind, but Vance continued before he could think of an order for them. "Wilburn had the ring first. Well, not first, but he had it right before Bart stole it from him and took it to Emma to be appraised. It's how she ended up with it after the bombing."

Instead of answering his questions, Vance was making more. Like where had the ring been before this? Why would a well-funded but stupid group be looking for it as well? And most importantly, how did Vance know all of this?

"When Gentry took the ring from my brother, there was a shit storm of backlash that has been hard for Wilburn to hide. Nine of his men have disappeared, and with them, one of my informants. I told you this was going to happen. But you didn't listen to me." Jorden looked at Vance when he told the man to shut up. "I need for you to bring me into what you know, Mr. McCade. This is most unfair of you when I have given you so much."

"And what is it you think you've helped me with? All I've gotten from you is information that I already had. The only reason that you're not dead yet is because I still have use for you. Now sit there and shut the fuck up before I take your tongue out and strangle you with it." Vance looked at him again, and Jorden had the most profound feeling that he wasn't making an idle threat to Richard. Then he grinned at him, and for reasons that he couldn't explain, he thought that his brother looked slightly deranged for a moment. "As I was saying. After Bart robbed Wilburn, he contacted Baldwin, Emma's grandfather, but we only just recently found out it was to threaten him about it. Until then we thought the two of them were working together, but as it turned out, the robbery was all Bart's doing, and lucky for us, Emma was there to intercede on the family's behalf."

"I don't think I understand." Vance nodded and told him he'd explain later. "And this man, he's here why? To try and get you to let him.... He planned to hold me until you did what he wanted."

"Pretty much. But what he didn't count on, and I need to talk with him about this, is that young Gavin was here and that he knows how to use a gun." So would Jorden. He'd not even known that the kid still had it. "But in this, it worked to our advantage. Richard is going to go home now, stay where he is supposed to, and not bother us again. I'm sure that he understands that to do so would get him as dead as the men he came here with."

Two men seemed to come out of the woodwork, dressed like Vance was most of the time, dark pants and shirts. Boots that looked as if they would kill as well as protect, and muscles that seemed almost fake; but Jorden knew that they were not. When Richard was taken away, Jorden watched Dalton leave as well with Gavin. He told him he'd be at the station with him.

"You have a lot of questions." Jorden nodded at Vance. "I'm sure you do. And I'll answer what I know. I've been meaning to talk to all of you about what I know, but I can start with you. I've been looking into the jewelry since Emma came to us."

"I got that part. But where I would like to start with is Richard, and why he thought that coming to get me would make you heel to him." Vance sat in the now vacant chair and said nothing. "Are you going to tell me or am I going to have to beat you to shit to get it out of you?"

"I don't think you'd want to tangle with me. I've been under some stress lately, and I don't want to have to hurt you. And I think you and I both know that I would." Jorden nodded. "When Emma came to us, I had already been working with someone on Gentry, her father. Not on the jewelry at that time, but drug deals, prostitution, as well as a long laundry list of shit he was claiming not to have anything to do with. There was speculation that he really was a good guy, as he was projecting, but there was a lot of shit going on within his organization that wasn't right. When Emma told me a few things about her brother, I went on that angle. That's when I found out about the robbery, as well as the man Bart had robbed. Her father really was a bad guy turned good, and the other stuff, the things that were illegal, that was all Bart."

"Glass...you're saying that Bart robbed Glass and took the ring. And when he took it to Emma to have it appraised, like she told us he did, he had no idea what he had." Vance nodded. "And these dots, I'm assuming that you've either connected them or are in the process of connecting them that will tell you where the other pieces are or where they might be. You have another picture, don't you? And this picture that he had, you talked to Jasmine about the brooch in it, didn't you?"

"Yes. You and I, along with the rest of the family, can see them for what they are. Not in the picture that Richard had, but this one." He pulled out a photo that was nearly the same as the one that Richard had, but not quite. "This is a picture of a drawing. It was found among some things at an estate sale about five years ago. You and I see a color photo with all the pieces laid out on a white background. Others, ones that have no magic, they see a drawing with just some cheap pieces of jewelry. It's rumored, and I have no way of knowing this for sure, that someone who is pure of heart, whatever the fuck that means, can see some of the designs but not all of it, not the magic part of it."

"How is that even possible?" Vance said he had no idea, but he wondered if the dragon knew. It took him several seconds to understand why he'd not just asked him. "You can't talk to him. I never...I guess I just assumed that since I could, anyone could. All right, I can ask. You think he might know something that can help us?"

"I don't have any idea. As you said, I can't talk to him. But you and Kenton can. And I think you'd be easier to get answers from because Kenton is...well, he's bossy, and would want more answers than I can give him. Or, he'd want to get into this with me and that might get him killed. These men are dangerous." Jorden nodded, picked up the photo that Vance had given him, and reached for the dragon. "Thank you. I need to see what I can find without worrying about what might befall the rest of the family."

I have seen that before, my lord. Not like this, but in a frame hanging on a wall. Jorden told his brother what the dragon said. *Long ago. Very long ago, the pieces were all together for a time. A man, long back in your lineage, he had paintings done with his five sisters wearing such pieces. But they fell on hard times. The family lost a great deal then, and the paintings, along with other items, were lost to him. Including his sisters, sadly.*

"There are six pieces. Not five." Jorden asked the dragon that when Vance mentioned it. "Which of the pieces wasn't painted?"

There were only five then. The necklace was a larger piece and was broken down when the lady who wore it said that it was too much for her. I had forgotten that until now. So with the permission of the dragon, it was broken into two pieces. A pair of torques were formed from one piece, then later made into a single one for the wearer. The necklace was made from the other piece, which is still large but manageable, I suppose. Both of them had to be together, the torques, in order for the magic to work, so it was worked so that they could forever be as one. Jorden asked him if he'd been the dragon. *Yes, in a small way. Each time one of the intended mates wears it and is…well, unable to connect, that is a good way to say it. But when one of them is unable in some way to go to the McCade dragons, then the dragon dies but for a spark of him. That is what I am now, just a spark that grows with each piece that is brought together.*

"So these paintings, they're of the women who wore them. But not the torques. I'm assuming that somewhere out there, someone owns these paintings and has hidden them away and forgotten them." Dragon told Jorden that was correct, but at some point, there had been several paintings of all the pieces with the woman. Jorden asked him if he knew where the paintings were.

No, I'm sorry. I have had no connection to the paintings, but I have heard that they are alive. Jorden was almost afraid to ask. Alive could mean all sorts of things, but he had a feeling it was just as he'd thought. They moved. But he had to know.

"Alive?" Dragon told him that each generation before the pieces were sold off would get together and have their portrait made with their husbands. And thusly, magical beings, like the ones that Vance had mentioned, would see it as it was. Dragons with their mates standing beside them. "You mean somewhere there are paintings of women with dragons, and the pieces that complete them?"

"The dragon would have been complete only in the first few, when all the pieces were together. After that, a single picture, painting, or whatever would have been made with each new bride. Again, the dragon would have been seen, but he would not be complete. Much like you are with only my heart beating in your chest to shift and the wings you can now use to fly." Jorden looked at his brother as he relayed the answer to him. "Yours and Lord Kenton's dragons would have wings, your body fully formed, if you were to be photographed now. But you'd not be whole. It would take all the pieces, all six of them, to make you whole and bring me to full life. And again, no one would see anything but a man near his bride. It would take someone magical to see either of you how you truly are."

"I'm more confused now than I was before this." Vance laughed at him. "Seriously, what could the other parts bring to the table that we might need? We can fly. Our bodies are dragon, and as Kenton found out at the hospital, we can breathe fire. What else is there?"

Each part of the set that is brought by your mates makes you more. The ring was your heart, the part of the dragon that brings him and me to life. The earrings, as you have discovered, brought you the wings so that you may have flight. The torques will give you strength in your arms and legs that will help you safeguard others. The necklace, a beautiful piece, will give your mind all manner of information, generations upon generations of all the McCades before you. There are the hair combs too, that will strengthen the blood that flows through your bodies. And in your mates'. It is said that once the pieces are together, the hair combs bring forth a dragon in the mates as well. Then there is the brooch.

"What does it do?" He felt the dragon shift along his body. Jorden thought that Vance had felt it as well, but before he could ask him about it, the dragon spoke again.

The brooch gives you armor. Stronger than the body you have with the dragon, and it will protect all that touch you. Even as men, you will be able to protect yourself with this piece of the demi parvure. It will not be seen by those that wish to breach it, but the magic will be powerful, consuming as well as deadly to your enemies.

Jorden looked at Vance as he told him what the dragon had said. They would be powerful; beyond that, they'd be nearly impossible to kill. Things ran though his head, not just questions—and there were plenty of those—but things that could happen to them should someone find out about it. What things someone with that kind of power could do to humans.

"And this Glass person. He wants the pieces. Why? He more than likely can't see them. He has no way of using the pieces, does he?" The dragon said no, no one but a McCade could ever use them. That was a relief. "Then why would he try to get them as his own? Blackmail? I can't believe that would be it. There must be something else."

There is, my lord. If a human, and he must be fully human, has even one of the pieces as his own, then he can command the dragon. Jorden was almost afraid to ask what he thought that might be. *He can control me. By owning the piece, he will own a part of me. When Emma was given the ring, it was from her brother to her, an inheritance. When Jasmine bought the box of junk and paid for them, she too owned me. She gave coin for it.*

"So as the women come here, they will have gotten the piece they bring in some way other than theft. If they don't, then the piece won't work." Dragon said that was correct. "Then if this Glass person takes it from someone, won't that, too, be a form of theft?"

Dragon didn't answer. Jorden wondered if he was thinking about his answer or just simply didn't know. Vance got up to pace but paused in front of the blank canvas. As he stood there staring at it, Jorden had an idea. He was going to paint them, all of them, on a single canvas, adding the women as they came. No one would know this but him, but he was going to do it. His mind was abuzz about how it would look when the dragon spoke.

I have checked the information that I have here. And so long as the piece is given to him by a man who steals it, and he does not murder to get it himself, then the piece is considered a gift to him. And should he pay the person to get the piece, it is a contract between them that has been fulfilled. Jorden told Vance what he'd been told. *I do not think I like this way of thinking.*

"Yeah, neither do I. So long as he doesn't steal it, he can pretty much...that's why Richard said he wanted to strike a bargain with me. He wants me to give him the piece I have. He doesn't know that they're a part of her." Vance said he thought that Wilburn did, but Richard didn't. More than likely it was something he was keeping from his brother. "So there is no trust between them either. Right?"

"I would say not. But this information, it gives me some things to consider. Like what if he were to take the piece that he wants...simply take it from the woman before she manages to make it her own? Is that the same thing? Does it not work?" Jorden said that he had no idea. "Me either."

Vance said he had some things to look into and would get back to him. When he left him there, Jorden looked at the canvas and decided it was too small for what he wanted it for, and started building one the way he wanted it. He was deep into his project when he felt Jasmine touch his mind.

Are you busy? There was panic there, not a lot but enough to have him moving toward the door. *I'm having some...I don't want to call them issues, but I might be in prison before the end of the day if you don't come here and rescue this fool in front of me. People who cheat others should have a special kind of hell, don't you think?*

He was laughing when he told her he was on his way. *Where are you, and what sort of weapon are you planning to use on this fool? And for the record, you should know that I've heard that a body can be incinerated with just a breath of air from my dragon should it come to that.*

Good to know. I'm at this auction house in town. I had no idea that there even was one, but I'm with your mom. By the way, she's not one to piss off, is she? He told her no, she wasn't. *Anyway, I'm here with her and Emma, and this jackass is trying to say that your mom broke this priceless piece. I told him that it's a knockoff, which it is, and he's calling the police. They're on their way, I guess.*

Dalton would be the one showing up, I'm betting. And he has Gavin. She asked him why. *I'll explain later. I'm on my way. Please don't kill anyone. And try to hold my mom back as well. She has a mean streak in her a mile wide. Just don't tell her I said that.*

He was nearly there when he saw the cruiser. It wasn't Dalton's, but he and Gavin were walking toward the man who worked for him along the modest size building that Jorden had completely forgotten about until Jasmine mentioned it. Once he spotted him, Dalton waited until he caught up before he asked what was going on. When they entered, Jorden thought about leaving again. This could not end well.

A…well, it looked to him like a mob had gathered. And they were no happier with what was going on than Jasmine and his mom seemed to be. As they made their way to the center of it all, he thought that he might need more money than he had to bail them all out.

"There you are." Jorden wasn't sure why he'd been pointed out by Mr. Wilson, but when he came toward him looking like a man on a mission, Jorden backed up. "You take this little woman of yours out of here right now and I won't press charges. The nerve of some people coming in here and calling me a fraud."

"I never said you were a fraud. You are, but I never said that." When he looked at Jasmine, she had her hands on her hips, her body stiff, and all he could think about was taking her home and fucking her brains out. "First you claim that my future mother-in-law broke this piece that you said you paid hundreds of dollars for. And by the way, if it's priceless, then hundreds of dollars won't cover it. And this break...how do you figure this is a fresh break when there is so much dust between the pieces of wood it's hard to see how they'd fit? Secondly, this is not old. Unless you count something from a few years ago as old. And which is it you're upset about? That it's priceless at hundreds of dollars? Broken today and that dust just happened to settle on it that fast? I'm confused as to what crap you're selling now."

"I bought this off of a reliable merchant, and they never sell me false goods." Mr. Wilson turned to Dalton now. "You arrest her right now. I want her arrested."

"On what charge?" Mr. Wilson started blustering about liars and cheats. "Well, those are good reasons not to deal with someone, but not one that would have me arrest her. You go on and get the receipt for that piece and I'll look it over. The other...well, you're on your own with that. However, I will tell you that if she proves to be right, then she can have you arrested for slander. If your reliable merchant sold you bad goods, now that I can take care of."

"I will not produce a receipt for this. I'm an honest man and I do honest sales." He looked around at the crowd that was beginning to look larger than when they had arrived. "I hold a sale here every week. You can ask these good people. Ask them if I don't sell good quality merchandise at a fair price here. I don't cheat them. Ask them. Any one of these good people know me."

"Two weeks ago, Hubert, you sold me a scale that was supposed to be from the thirties. It's not true in its calibrations, and when I talked to you about it, you said that I'd already paid for it and I must have done something to it." Mr. Wilson waved off the dissatisfied customer. "Yeah, that's about the way you did me before."

"I got a few pieces of graniteware here a month or so ago. I was told that it's from the same time period. You even showed me in a catalog where it was three hundred dollars. When I got it home, I found out that the chipping on it, which you called wear, was done recently, and that the same set sells at the local camping store for ten bucks. I think you'd even tried to glue some of it back on when it caused a hole as big as my thumb to come through."

Mr. Wilson started making excuses as more and more people began to bring up complaints.

Jorden made his way to Jasmine. "You want to own an antique store? I think we can get you some merchandise fairly cheap if you think you can sell this stuff." She looked at him then around the room. He could see her mind working on how much the furniture and other items were worth that had been hanging on the wall since he'd been a kid. She asked him how high she could go. "You know what this is worth a hell of a lot better than I do. You deal with him and we'll go from there." She asked him if he was sure and for an answer, he kissed her.

"Mr. Wilson, do you want to sell out? I mean, all of this. Do you want to get out of the selling business?" He turned and looked at Jasmine when she spoke. "I'll give you fair price for all of this, excluding the building. I have no use for it. And I mean fair, not what you think of as fair."

Mr. Wilson asked her if she was kidding. She said she

never kidded about money, nor antiques. He then took a look around, his mind working on how much he could over inflate things, Jorden had no doubt. When he looked at the crowd, he could see that he wasn't going to get help from them. Nor likely any more business would be coming from them.

"How much?" Jasmine said it didn't work that way, he was to give her a price and she'd work from there. "I'd have to have a lot. I've been collecting the stuff in here for years. This here is my livelihood. It's not going to be cheap."

"How much?" He could see that she was good at this. And that she was enjoying it. "I don't think you can count on this being much of a money maker for you, once word gets out how upset everyone is on some of your...sales. You tell me what you want, and as I said, I'll see."

He gave a price, fifty grand. It was much less than he'd thought he'd say, and Jorden was ready to say he'd take it. But the hand on his shoulder, his mom's hand, kept him quiet. Jorden watched Jasmine work Mr. Wilson. It was like watching a professional negotiate down a jumper.

"I'll give you fifteen. There is a lot of just junk in here filling in space where you could have nice pieces. Fifteen grand. And I'll even move the crap out that I don't have any use for." Mr. Wilson snorted at her and told her she was nuts. "I'm betting that in a few weeks, less, the bank will take what I offer them. Maybe I should just wait for them. What do you think, Jorden?"

"What do you mean, the bank? I have a good standing with my bank." Jasmine picked up the unopened mail that was laying right in front of them. The words past due were stamped in red on the front of it. There were several more, all of them with some marking that said he wasn't as flush as he was claiming. Mr. Wilson snatched it back. "I've made me some arrangements on that. You can buy it off me for forty grand."

"Twenty, or I wait for the sale." Mr. Wilson was pissed. "Up to you, but if you take my money now you can walk away with a little cash. And be free and clear. You know as well as I do that if the sale from the bank doesn't get enough cash, you still owe it. Trust me when I tell you, I'm going to get it for a great deal less than you need to cover taxes and other crap that you're behind on."

"I dislike you a great deal." He put out his hand. "Twenty. And I don't want to hear from a single person how you ran things into the ground."

Jasmine looked at Jorden and he nodded. She took Mr. Wilson's hand and shook it. Christ, he'd just bought twenty grand worth of old shit. And for less than half the price he would have paid for it.

"Thank you." She kissed him on the mouth and he thought he would gladly have paid more if she did that again. "I am going to make you so much money that I'll have you paid back in a year."

Before he could tell her that she wasn't going to pay him back, she walked away talking to some of the other patrons in the building. His mom kissed him on the cheek and told him he'd done a good thing.

"She's not going to pay me back, Mom." She told him he'd better let her. "Why? It's not like I can't afford this. And she will be happy here. And that alone is worth more than she got him to take for the place."

"Yes, she will be happy, but I have news for you. See those two pieces over there in the corner?" He looked. One of them was a white cupboard like he'd seen in a million other homes, and the other was a tall dresser, taller, he thought, than he was.

"Mr. Wilson has two hundred on the cupboard and Jasmine said she could get twelve hundred easy. And the tall boy, the dresser…he has fifty on it. She said she has a buyer right now that would pay six grand for it. Your future wife? She is going to be making a mint in no time. And if you really want her happy, then I would suggest that you take the money that she pays you back and put it in an account for your son. He's going to need help when he finally gets to go to college."

Okay, maybe he'd not come out so badly. He started looking around at some of the other items in a new light. Yes, they'd have to clean the furniture up, get rid of a lot of the junk, or what he thought was junk, but she would be happy, and that above all else was worth every penny.

CHAPTER 7

Wilburn set the phone down on the cradle and thought about what he'd just found out. The piece of jewelry that he'd stolen last month was a fake. His men had gone into the house and gotten just what he'd sent them for, so technically, it wasn't their fault, but someone was going to have to pay for this, and he was in the mood to make someone, anyone really, pay big time. He looked at the picture again, the one that he'd stolen from his grandda all those years ago, and wondered not for the first time what it was about these pieces that had people thinking they were worth more than they were. Even without the added knowledge of the dragons, people were going nuts about them.

"Why are you forsaking me?" The picture, of course, had no answer, and he laid it down. Twice now, two times in the last month, he'd been on a wild goose chase. He looked at Richard when he laughed. "What is it? You're no more help than the picture is."

"No, but I did get something you didn't know. I know that one of them McCades has more information than even we do. I'm telling you, that younger man, he knows a lot." Wilburn asked him what he could know. "Well, he did know that all the pieces have to be together to work. And that the picture that we have isn't a true adaptation of what it looks like. Also, they figured out the connection to you and the ring. Nasty business that. You should have been more careful. Now they can connect you to Bart, and we all know how that might turn out, don't we?"

Wilburn might have to end up killing his brother before long. He was helping him by keeping tabs on the McCades, but lately it seemed as if he was keeping things from him. Wilburn wasn't sure what it might be, but he knew that he was.

"You said that there are five pieces. They have two now. If we can't find the other pieces before they do, then we're pretty much fucked. I need at the rest of it or we'll never be able to control the dragon." Richard nodded but said nothing. "Do you know where the last three pieces are?"

"No. Can't say that I do. But they don't either, so that's fine for now." He was going to die today, Wilburn thought. The fucker was lying to him about how many pieces there were, and he knew it. "And there are six pieces, not five. I heard that painter telling his brother about that. I don't know what it would be; they seemed to have all the pieces a woman might want to doll herself up with now, so we'll have to think on that one."

So he did come clean on this. But Wilburn thought he was still keeping things from him. He had told him about the bug he'd planted in the painter's building, but he wouldn't let him listen in on the conversations there. Wilburn, of course, never mentioned that he had his own bugs in the building and had heard the entire exchange too. Most of it anyway. Wilburn was going to have to have someone go in and check on the device he had and its placement. Something was very off about the sound at times.

Richard had also told him that there was a boy there, useless for the most part, but Wilburn knew for a fact that he'd gotten the drop on his brother, and that wasn't good. He'd held him until the police got there. He also knew that Richard had lost him six of his men by fucking with the family before he'd told him to. Not great men, but good men that were helpful in tracking down things for him. Like the fucking pieces that kept eluding him.

"I've been thinking about a part of the recording that I can't listen to." Wilburn asked his brother what he meant. "As I was listening in on them, at one point, they started talking about the picture and how it was a fake. Then their words sort of got fuzzy. Like there was a lawnmower running in the room with them. No matter how much I tried, I just couldn't understand a word they were saying."

"Do tell." It was the same thing that he'd heard too when he'd tried to listen in. As if someone had turned a blocker on so that they could have a conversation without anyone eavesdropping. In order for that to happen, they would have to know about the bugs, which he was sure that no one did. "Are you sure that you got it planted well? That maybe it didn't fall and get stepped on?"

"No, no, it was right under the table where he has all that material laying. I had to ask one of the men what that might have been. I guess he stretches his own canvas for some reason. Seems like a lot of work when you can just go buy it. Anyway, it was right there, stuck really well too. And I heard them talking after I left, then...well, then the lawnmower started up. And later on, it was clear again. I could hear music playing, softly like. The only sound that wasn't music was a click-click noise that I wasn't sure what it was until later." Richard nodded as if he was verifying himself. "It was as if the lawnmower was shut off and there wasn't anything but this plucking noise. Like a stapler, but one of those great big ones. And I might not have thought of that, but I did see one of them on his table."

"So something or someone is blocking your bugging of his office. Do you have any planted elsewhere? Other than the artist's building?" Richard said it was his first one, but he had plans of getting one into the police station this week. "That's right, you mentioned that. That other McCade, he's a cop. You think that's smart? I mean, a bug in there is really bad if you're caught."

"I won't get caught. And even if they do find it, they already think I'm working with the one boy, so it's doubtful that they'll think I'm in on it. Vance. You know, he's sort of scary. Have you ever talked to him?" Wilburn said he'd not had the pleasure. "Not much of a pleasure, I'm afraid. One time he threatened to cut my twig and berries off and feed them to me. I had no idea what that was and nearly agreed with him. Might have too, if he hadn't looked so pissed off at the time. But then, now that I think on that, he's pretty much like that all the time. Anyway, I asked Rebecca about it and she said it was my dick and balls. Another time, he said that—"

"I really don't care what sort of threats he lays at your doorstep, Richard. What is it you've been able to figure out about what their plans are?" Richard was annoying as fuck, and most of the time he screwed things up for him. Usually he didn't want to kill him with every beat of his heart, but he thought he would gladly do so today. "And when do you meet with this cowboy that you've been working with."

"Cowboy? I don't know that any of them could be considered a cowboy. Why would you even...? Ah, you're making a funny. I don't know. I'm supposed to wait for him to call me. But usually if I don't hear from him in a few days, I go to him. I think he forgets about me at times." Wilburn didn't think that was it at all, but said nothing. "He has it in his head that I'm not very useful to him."

"Are you? Because from where I'm sitting, you're not too terribly useful to me." Richard said he was more useful than he was getting credit for. "I just bet you are. When you hear from him again, let me know. I want to also know when you plant those other bugs. No chance of you getting into the houses, is there? I'm sure we can get a lot of information from there."

"No, no. I can't go there. He told me—and I do believe him—that if I went there, he'd kill me. Nothing else, just if I showed up at his home or those of his family, I'm dead. Like I said, he's scary when he wants to be." No one was that scary, Wilburn thought, but said nothing more to his brother.

A bit later, Richard left and Wilburn was alone to think. Had Bart just left things alone, then he'd have the piece that he needed. But because of his inability to leave things alone that didn't belong to him, Wilburn no longer had the one key that would control a dragon. A fucking dragon. But the fucker had gotten himself dead, and it had taken Wilburn nearly a month to figure out the connection to the doctor marrying, and that he'd married Bart's sister, of all people. And that she'd had the ring.

Of course, Wilburn stole things as well, but that was beside the point. Bart had fucked him over without even knowing it. The money—and there had been a great deal of it—had been bad enough, but the ring too? That had been a real bitch. And

105

Wilburn hadn't had the opportunity to kill the little fucker. He'd done that all by himself. And the McCades had gotten their first piece of the pie.

When his phone rang he just let the service pick it up. Wilburn rarely answered his own phone, even his cell, unless he was expecting someone to call him with information. When the ringing was cut off, he thought about the piece that he'd gotten tested today. He'd thought he had the necklace.

He looked at his picture. There was the ring and earrings that he'd marked off. Those were gone to him. The necklace was there, and he had put a small mark near it that he'd have to remove now. Along with the hair combs and brooch, he had to wonder what the sixth piece was. Couldn't think of a single thing that a woman would want to put on and bring a dragon to life. Now that he was sure there was another piece, he started looking for what it might be.

Two hours after his brother left him, Wilburn had several items on a sheet of paper of what the last piece might be. Not much to go on, not really, but it was a start. As he began digging deeper into what it might look like besides having something to do with a dragon, there was a knock at his door. He looked up when Quincy asked if he had a moment.

"You find anything out?" He said that he'd been looking, and all he could come up with was that another piece might have been found in California. "You go out there and have a look. Do you know what this piece might be?"

"The man who owned the house it was supposed to be in is a man by the name of Tucker, a John Tucker. Several years ago, before his wife passed away, he told one of his grandsons that he had a prize, and that someday he'd be a billionaire. And that he'd be riding on the backs of dragons. The kid, I guess, didn't take him very seriously until he came across a receipt for a dragon brooch. So far he's not seen anything like that, and is having the house torn apart looking for it. I guess his grandfather had paid over six million for the thing, and he wants it found." This was good information, but he didn't bother telling the kid that. He wanted him to work harder. "I'll head out there now."

When he didn't move, Wilburn had a feeling that he wanted money, a lot of it. But he wasn't going to give him any, and if the kid proved to be too greedy, he'd just send someone else out there and Quincy's body would never be found.

"There's something else." Wilburn waited for him to continue, and when it looked like he wasn't going to, Wilburn started to tell him to get on with it. But Quincy looked at him then. "The man, Tucker, he had a list. The grandson told me that it had a word next to each of the names on the list. And with the one that said brooch, it said Tucker. The other names, ones that he said he'd never heard of before, were crossed out and the word dead beside each of them, with a date."

"So? He had a list of who owned what piece of this puzzle. See if you can get the list and we'll figure it out." Quincy nodded then shook his head. "I don't have time for games, boy. What is it?"

"All the people on the list, his grandfather included, died within five to seven days of each other." The chill that went up Wilburn's back scared him just a little. "I'm not sure that getting that list is a good idea, do you? I mean, a week apart? What are the odds of that happening? And is it the dragon doing it?"

He was gone before Wilburn could say anything. He might have been gone for a few minutes to over an hour, but Wilburn's mind was working details. Who was on the list? How had they died? Did they have a piece? And if so, where was it now? After the kid had mentioned the dragon killing off people, Wilburn had gone into a sort of mental question session. All questions, no answers, however. All his mind could circle around was, perhaps it was the dragon that was taking care that he didn't get his piece. Was that even possible?

Bart was dead. His dad and grandda as well. All the people he had sent to get the fucking earrings were dead. He'd had most of those killed himself, but they were gone all the same. The only people around that had any direct contact with the jewelry were the women who now wore it, and they were a part of this shit going on. Maybe he had to rethink this. Perhaps send someone there to find the brooch that he could sort of trust. Maybe he'd send Richard after it.

~~~

Jasmine was in the middle of taking a good inventory of the crap she'd gotten when she felt something. She wasn't entirely sure what it might have been…a movement? Maybe, but that didn't seem right. A noise? No, it couldn't be that, because the music playing in the room with her would have canceled out anything that she might have heard. Standing up, careful of where she was, Jasmine went to find Gavin, who was working in the back of the building.

She had ten days to get the stuff out of the building. Mr. Wilson—Hubert, he'd ask her to call him—had come by the police station that morning and told Dalton that the owner of the building wanted it cleaned out. He had taken a great deal of satisfaction in telling Dalton that, but she'd already been moving things around anyway. It was just a matter of moving faster now.

Gavin met her in the short hall and put his finger to his lips. She nodded and asked him if they were in danger, and he smiled. No, she supposed not, and moved behind him when he pointed into the large room where the furniture that she'd already decided to keep was sitting. There in the middle of it was the biggest fox she'd ever seen.

"How did it get in here?" she asked Gavin in a whisper. He said he thought it had been in here for a while…he seemed pretty comfortable with things. "Is he real?"

Neither one of them could tell the difference between a shifter and an animal. Not as yet anyway. Jorden said he'd try to teach her, but he'd been holed up in his studio for two days now and she hated to bother him. When she felt a small touch to her mind, she stiffened until she knew who it was. Kenton.

I have two of those big dolly things you asked for. I'm going to bring them by on my…. What is it? Is someone there with you? I can be there in ten minutes. Call to —

We have a fox in the building, and we were just trying to figure out if he is a shifter or just a fox. He asked her what color he was. *Red. I'm assuming that you know a fox shifter.*

Yes. A family of them, as a matter of fact. You do as well. Maxwell and Abby Fox, as in what they are. She decided that she didn't like him very much. *Just go where he can see you. If it's Maxwell, he more than likely already knows you're staring at him.*

She told Gavin who it was and he whistled. When Maxwell, if it was him, turned and looked at them, Abby came into the room with a large picnic basket. She was just a person, thankfully, and smiled at them. Waving them down, she told Kenton that was who it was.

As they made their way to the couple, Gavin was going on about how he'd felt the man shift. That might have been what she felt too, and asked him how he knew. He just grinned at her, and she knew she was going to be upset for some reason.

"Vance bit me." She asked him why he'd do a fool thing like that. "Because he said that if I was ever lost or hurt, he'd be able to find me faster. And he said that if I was really smart, I'd let a few other people that he knew do the same. He told me that Dad can find you easily enough, but the rest of them might have some trouble."

"I see." She really didn't, but decided to ask someone about it. Not Vance. While she liked him a great deal, he scared the shit out of her. There was a quiet deadliness about him that made her think that he was forever watching a person to see where he could stick a knife. Maybe not her, but she didn't think she was far off the mark about him. "The next time you have someone bite you, could you ask me about it first? I might not want them knowing where you are all the time."

Abby said that Maxwell had decided to have a little sniff around. Not that he expected to find anything like foul play on any of the merchandise, but it was a game he loved to play when he had free time. Apparently Maxwell considered himself quite the detective. When he joined them for the lunch they'd brought in, she asked him about his finds.

"Nothing much. The big dresser there, the one with the mirror, it's been in the home of someplace where perfume was spilled on it. A great deal of it." Jasmine told him that according to the paperwork she'd been able to match up to it, the dresser, along with a chair that she'd not been able to locate just yet, had come from a brothel. "Well, that explains the other scents. A great many males have…well, it was touched a great deal by men."

They laughed at his obvious embarrassment. She told him about some of the things she'd been able to unearth. "I've also found a lot of books in the back. I don't think that Hubert knew their worth. There are two first editions that I've found, as well as a few signed books that I'm going to have to find the author." Abby told her about the author that had come through town about thirty years or so ago. "Do you remember his name? I might have some of his work. There are a lot of books by him that are about this area."

"No, child, I can't remember. But I'm sure that Aisha might. I think she might have put him up for a couple of days. He was a nice man, down on his luck. I believe that he might have paid his way through here with copies of his books." Jasmine made a mental note to ask her. "Before I forget, a nice sized box arrived for you today. I guess it was forwarded here from your old place. I'm not sure how they connected your home there to this one, but it's still out in the garage. They arrived just as we were leaving the house."

It wasn't until the couple was gone that she thought about the box. It would be nice to have something from their own home, and she was excited to go and open it. But as she was reaching for her notebook, something occurred to her. Their house had burned to the ground. There wouldn't have been anything left. Not to mention, as Abby had said, how did whoever sent it here know where she was? Getting up slowly, she went to find Gavin. He was going through some boxes of comic books that she'd found, and only had to look at her to become worried.

"I need for you to do me a favor and not leave here." He nodded and asked her what was going on. "I'm not sure, but it's about that box. I think something is wrong with it, it's not safe. If I know that you're here, I don't have to worry about whether or not you can be hurt or something."

"Because the house burned down." She nodded. "Mom, Uncle Vance knows that I'm upset. He wants to know what's going on. He's talking to me from this connection that we have because of the bite he took."

"Tell him...." She wasn't sure what to tell him. The truth?

Maybe, but what if he was hurt from whatever it was? But if she lied to him, he'd more than likely know that too. She decided that the truth was easier to figure out for him. "Tell him what we've just figured out." She watched her son, all she had left in this world that was hers. When he nodded to her, she felt better knowing that he was on her side.

"He said for us to stay here, and that he's having Dalton and Dad come here too. He also said that his mom will be here as well...they were having lunch, and she's going to hang out with us. All right?" She hated to interrupt his time with his mom. "Mom, he said that he's going to have a team go and have a look at the box, and the inside of the house too."

The McCade men had lunch with their mom at least once a week if they could, and they all met on Sunday evening for a family dinner. She and Gavin had been excited to join them this time.

Jorden joined them a few minutes later. Dalton said that he was going to have someone search the other houses, as well as any places that someone might think they had a connection to. The first place on the list was Jorden's studio. It only took them five minutes to find the bug and figure out the fingerprints on it. The second bug in his studio was a little harder to find, but no less scary. Someone had been listening in on them.

They were still going over the furniture that she was having moved when Jorden told her that Vance was coming here with Kenton. Emma was with them as well, and she was fired up. Jasmine asked him about what.

"Apparently she got a box as well. It was addressed to Emma with one 'm,' but she didn't see it on the stoop until one of Vance's team came to talk to Kenton. They haven't opened either of them yet, but Vance has some questions for you." She nodded. "We're fine, honey. No one is going to hurt us."

But they were trying to was all she could think about. Someone was trying to hurt her and Emma. And had she not been here when the box was delivered, she might well have opened it without thinking. Emma might not have…she had the mind of a criminal. Not in a bad way, but she was forever thinking outside the box. Jasmine decided that she was going to do a bit of that on her own. It might well save her new family's life.

The box had been ready to explode had she opened it. Emma's as well, but the amount of explosive material in Jasmine's would have taken out the front of the house as well as part of the garage. When she sat down, Jorden held her hand while Vance told her all of it. The prints on the box matched the one on the second bug in Jorden's office.

"So you know who it might be?" Vance nodded. "Does that mean you go out there and arrest him or something?"

"Or something. But for now we're going to leave the bugs where they are." She asked him why he'd do that. "Because they're not aware that we know, and it's better to have a bug in your offices than a bomb in the garage. The bug, while annoying, won't take out all my manly parts when I get too close to it."

"You're sick, did you know that?" He laughed at her. "Won't they think it odd that the box didn't do what it was supposed to do? Like kill us?"

"You're not home." She said she knew that. "What I mean is, neither you nor Emma have been home all day. That will buy us at least a few hours to figure out a plan, execute it, and do something to the bad guy."

"Do I want to know what that might be?" Vance said nothing. She thought maybe she might like his silence over telling her the gory details. "You bit my son. To find him.

Would he really benefit if he had more people that could find him? Like some of your team?"

"Yes. But if you don't mind, I'd very much like to decide who does it." She nodded. At this point, she'd about agree to anything so long as they were safe. "Also, if you would be so kind as to let me as well as a few others have a little taste of your blood, we'd feel a great deal better."

"Yes. Right now I'm so afraid that I'd even let the president have a little bite." He assured her that as a mated cat, his wife would be very upset about that. "The president is a shifter? Who else? The pope?"

"No, not the pope. But there are quite a few in offices right now. Not so many around here, but there are a few." Jasmine didn't want to think about that and told him so. "You will be better at this once you are around us more."

"Will I be? Around you more? Because I don't want to be killed. And it's looking to me like some dick wants me six feet under a great deal." Vance assured her that she'd be around for a long time if she paid attention to her surroundings. "Thank you, I will from now on. And you take care of my son." He told her he would. Jasmine hoped so. She couldn't lose him. Any of them.

CHAPTER 8

Aisha wanted to hug the young man, but she was also trying to wait for him to come to her. Gavin was a good boy; scary smart, it seemed, but nice and very polite. And today he was spending the day with her while his mom organized the move into the new building. When he sat across from her, she handed him the list of names and explained what she was doing. Maybe, she thought, he'd help her out a little too.

"These are the names of the people that have paid to have dinner at the Mother's Ball. Can you help me put their names around tables?" He asked her what sort of order they went in, and she told him instead what they were doing. "Every year, as you've heard, we have this charity event to raise money for different projects in town. Mothers down on their luck who might need help with the rent. Or a child that has no coat or school supplies. The fund is there for them to use. Of course we run out very quickly nowadays, but we can help a few people."

"Mrs. McCade, you're saying these people overpay to eat at this dinner thing, and you use the money for the underprivileged. Is that all?" Aisha asked him what he meant. "I mean, you just have a dinner for them. And that money— I'm assuming that it's more than a burger price—is what you use to help people. And that building that we helped you look for? It looks like the school lunchroom where I went to school. Can't you get something, I don't know, prettier for this?"

"If I do then we have to use some of the money that would go for the children. Believe me, I've thought of that too. We have about seventy-five people pay a hundred dollars a plate. To be honest with you, less and less are showing up. I'm betting you can help me with that. What did you have in mind? And before you answer that, I want you to know that you're now a part of this, being a McCade." He nodded and smiled at her, and Aisha fell right over in love with the boy. Looking down at the list, she could hardly see it for the tears. But it was him calling her Mrs. McCade that got her going. "Gavin, you're a wonderful young man, but if you continue to call me Mrs. McCade, I might make you in charge of this thing."

He laughed, such a wonderful free sounding sound. "I've talked to Mom about it. And you know that I lost my grannie not long ago." She told him again she was sorry about that. "Me too. She wasn't...I loved her very much, but she was older than you and she wasn't in the best of health. Besides, you're fun. I don't mean that Grannie wasn't fun, but she was more of a quiet fun, I guess."

"Thank you. I'm very spry for my age. And raising six boys all by myself made me very quick on my feet." He laughed with her. "You don't have to call me Grandma, but Aisha would be nice."

"I'd like to do that." She nodded. "I call Jorden Dad now, and the others Uncle. If you'd not mind me calling you Grandma, then I'd very much like that." She nodded and had to wipe at the tears. "Mom told me that you'd be my step-grandma, but she didn't think you'd ever treat me that way. The step part, I mean."

"You tell your mother she's brilliant, and I love her as well." He nodded and looked at the charts. It was time to change the subject matter or she'd be sobbing like a baby. "I have them all in order there. Friends and family together with people they know well. They seem to enjoy that."

"Why?" She said that was the way they did it. "Okay, but sometimes maybe they're sick of their friends. I don't have a lot of them—being a nerd does that for me—but I would think if you sort of mixed it up a bit, people might have more friends when they left."

She just stared at him. The kid was right. She was usually so bored at this thing because she knew all the stories of the people she sat with. Picking up the list, she looked it over and told him he was right. In ten minutes they'd cut all the names from the sheet and were taping them to the tables in no particular order. No one was spared…even spouses were separated.

"What else did you have in mind?" He looked at her when she asked. "You had an idea for us to make more money. What is it?"

"An auction." She told him she didn't have anything to do that with. "No, but there are merchants in town who could donate. Grocery stores could give gift cards. Mom, I bet she'd give you something to auction off. And Aunt Emma, if she were to bake a bunch of those cookies she does and box them up pretty, someone would pay to get those. Too much, but it's all a tax write off anyway, right? Even a different place to hold it. If you asked someone, say the guy that has the big barn out of town, if you could use it and tell him what you're using it for, he'd let you. Might even help you decorate it up so it looks less like a barn and more festive."

He got up then and left her there. An auction? How did one even go about getting that organized? And she knew Roger Gent. He was a nice man that had had that barn built when his eldest daughter had been married. They'd used it for the reception. And it had been prettied up too. When Gavin returned, he had some papers in his hand. He told her what he'd been able to figure out. She quickly read it over and looked at him. The kid was going to go far, she knew it.

"Will you help me? I mean, it says here that when you get people to donate, you should pick them up in person and give them a thank you note." He made another suggestion. "Yes, I like that. Their picture on the gift along with their store front is an excellent idea. And if we can get some nicer gifts — I'm not saying we will — but we might be able to sell more tickets for this thing as well."

"I don't see why not. And you're making all the flowers, right?" She told him it took her days to get them together. "Why not let one of the local florists do it? And then give them away at the end of the dinner. This article I read about it said that florists have contests within their own shops that one of their employees might win as best table decoration. Grandma, you need to delegate more, I think."

He was right. Not just on the delegation part, but how to make this charity event more of a fun thing rather than just a boring dinner. As they pulled out phones and started making lists, she realized that she and Gavin were having a blast. Within an hour she was getting very excited. They had twenty donations that varied from gift cards to a full day at the spa. She had him call Emma and ask her about the baked goods.

When he laughed and put the phone on speaker, she

thought for sure that Emma was going to tell them they were nuts. But the girl was laughing harder than Gavin was, and she wanted to tell him to cut it off, they'd do something else.

"I was thinking that instead of cookies from me, how about cakes auctioned off by the women in the groups?" Aisha looked at Gavin as she continued. "They bake up their best cake and put it in a pretty basket to be auctioned off. I saw that on a movie once; it was picnic baskets, but this could be fun too. I'm going to bake some scones and other sweets to raffle off too, but I think if you get the community involved like that and what Gavin has suggested, this might be the hit of the year."

When Jasmine and Jorden joined them a bit later, they not only had a list of places that were donating items to be raffled off, but had sold over sixty more tickets to the dinner. All in all, it was a very profitable day for the charity.

"I can't believe this. All because you made a simple suggestion. Gavin, I love you to pieces." When she hugged him to her, he wrapped his arms around her tightly. Aisha thought it was one of the best hugs she'd ever had. Hugging him back, she looked at her son. Jorden had given her this. Him and his new mate.

Before she could burst into tears, because as surely as she was standing there, she knew that she was, Aisha moved into the kitchen and leaned against the door. When she looked at Meggie, her long time cook, she just shook her head and left her as well. Aisha loved her family so much.

~~~

The man standing in front of her building gave her pause. Jasmine thought about walking by, just pretending that she wasn't headed to the antique store, but he saw her and smiled. For some reason she didn't think of friendship. More like he

119

was the big bad wolf and she was lunch.

He isn't human. Dragon told her to cross the street. *Hurry. I feel danger from him, and I believe him to have anger in his heart.*

She was nearly across the street when he called out to her. Going faster, keeping an eye on him, Jasmine screamed when someone grabbed her left arm. The man, a stranger too, pressed something over her mouth and nose and she knew she was a goner. Reaching to Jorden, all she was able to say was *danger* before everything blacked out.

Waking up, she knew that she'd been put somewhere damp. The ground beneath her not only felt like dirt, but it was cold as well. When she started to sit up, Jasmine realized that not only were her hands tied, but her feet as well. And there was something across her mouth. Rolling to her side, she tried to get her bearings.

My lady, you must be very still. I know not how badly you are hurt. She told dragon she didn't hurt, but almost as soon as she said it to him, she began to feel every muscle protest. *They have tossed you around as if you are nothing. I have told the others, Kenton and Jorden, that you are awake as well.*

Do you know where I am? He said that he did not. *Can I talk to Jorden or one of the others?*

Jorden said that he has tried several times to reach you and cannot. He believes that you are in some sort of deep hole, or that you are being shielded from him. Lord Kenton is having no more luck. She asked if Gavin was all right. *Yes. As soon as I realized that you were taken, I contacted Jorden and he gathered the young man up.*

At least he was safe. *Do you have any idea who those men were? I'm assuming that they want the earrings, right?*

That is what we are thinking. You are well then? I am to tell Jorden how you are faring. I do not think he believes me when I said you were unharmed. Jasmine laughed. *I will tell him you have not lost your sense of humor, shall I?*

Yes, tell him that and tell him that I love him and I really am doing well. Jasmine told the dragon that she was tied up and gagged and to let them know that. *Also, there is dirt under me. I can't see any walls as yet. So I'm thinking that there is either no electricity in this building or I'm in a cave as they think.*

She could hear noises but not what they were. It sounded like a cat with their tail in a wringer, something her grannie had said all the time. It wasn't until she'd explained that old washers had a ringer on the top of them to squeeze out the water from the clothing rather than a spin cycle that she got it. Jasmine missed her more and more daily.

Mistress, Kenton has suggested that you try to smell things. I told him that you might not be able to smell much as you are gagged, but he assures me that you would be able to smell with your nose, not only your mouth as I can. Jasmine felt a little burble of laughter escape around the gag and thanked the dragon for that. *It is my pleasure. But can you help them in this? He assures me that it will be most helpful if you can narrow things down for them to find you.*

Inhaling deeply, all she could smell was tape. But when she tried to separate that smell from the other things, she could smell a man's cologne as well as iron, like old water in an iron pail or something. Telling the dragon that and the noise that she could hear, Jasmine waited for some feedback.

Everyone just refers to you as the dragon or Dragon. Do you have a name? He asked her what she meant. *I mean, I'm Jasmine, my son is Gavin, what is your name? Surely there is something more than just the dragon or Dragon.*

I have been called Dragon forever, my lady. There was a time when I was called the McCade Dragon. Not me, in fact, but one of my ancestors that lived with them as a dragon. If it would help you, I can be called what the first of the McCades was called. A great and powerful name it was. She asked him what it was. *His name was Caelin. It is an Irish name that means powerful warrior. He was, according to records, both. He had three wives, each of them bearing him a daughter, but he never gave up on having a son when they died so young. Then late in his life, his wife, older than most at that time to be giving birth, gave him a son. This son became the one who came up with the idea to have the dragon move into the jewels to be safe from mankind.*

What a sad story. I'm glad that he got himself a son, but that is no less tragic, don't you think? But I like the name. That is what we will call you from now on. Caelin, the McCade Dragon. I like that. He told her that she humbled him. *No, you're going to save us. And my ass right now. Do we have anything yet?*

She heard the voice before she got an answer from Caelin. There was a bright light, making her close her eyes against it, and then it was out. Not moving at all, she waited for someone to say something. It was then that she smelled the man's cologne. It was the same as she had smelled on the tape.

When one of them spoke, she decided that she needed to remember his voice in the event that he got away and she had to identify him. The second man spoke as well, and it was all she could do not to turn and look at him. It was Vance, she'd bet her life on it. But she kept her eyes closed, trying to pretend that she was still out.

"I told you. He's kidnapped her and plans to do all sorts things to her to get the earrings." A finger touched her cheek and she thought it might be Vance as the other man continued. "He sent one of his flunkies out to California too. He was telling me how he came across another piece of the pie. Why pie? Anyway, he sent that boy out there who doesn't know shit about things the way you and I do."

"And this boy, does he know that you're helping me?" Vance put his fingers over her eyes then touched her mind. *Stay still. Nothing is going to hurt you. This fool thinks that he can get me to play him against his brother. But no harm will come to you.*

He's the bastard that brought me here. He said he'd already figured that out. *Oh. Well then, why aren't you getting me out of here?*

Because I need more than just this dumbass in this. He is playing me against his brother, as I said, but I don't know why yet. Not that they're both not going to be going to prison, but for now, I need more information. Such as, is there really a piece out in California? It could save a woman's life to know that. She told him good idea. *Yeah, I have them on occasion. In a moment, I'm going to drop a knife behind you. When you get it, please be careful. It's very sharp.*

"When is your brother supposed to come here and get her? I'm assuming that he is aware that someone kidnapped her already." Vance spoke to the other man, and it took Jasmine a few seconds to realize it wasn't her he was asking. The other man said that his brother was aware, and that he expected him and an extraction team soon to get her. "You mean to cut her ears off. I'm to understand that is the only way to get them, correct?"

"So far as we know. If she had just left them in the box where she was supposed to, then we'd not...my brother wouldn't have had to go this far. I think he has it in his head that he only needs the one piece to rule, or something like that." Vance said nothing, but she heard a soft thud and something heavy touched her hand. His *be careful* was all she got before the bright light flashed once again and a door closed.

She touched her fingers to the object by her hand and

nearly screamed when it cut her. As blood filled her palm, she tried to be extra careful in getting it turned around so that she could cut whatever binding she had on her wrist.

After painfully stabbing herself twice more, she got her hands free. When she sat up, still in the dark, she peeled the gag off her mouth and stretched her jaw twice before moving to free her legs. Jasmine had to sit there for a couple of minutes, just rubbing the blood back to her feet and hands, before she felt like she could stand without falling over. When she stood up, carefully, Jasmine was terrified that she was going to get killed as soon as she left the little room.

The door opened silently, and when she was in the big room beyond, her eyes burned with the light. Jasmine then looked down at her hands and realized she really had done a number on herself. One of the cuts looked like she might need to get some stitches. But that was the least of her problems if she was caught here. Moving along the wall toward the windows, Jasmine tried to reach Jorden. Relief at hearing his voice nearly took her to her knees.

Thank God. Where are you? Do you know? And are you hurt? She might have laughed at his tone had she not been trying to figure out the answers to the questions that he was rapidly firing at her. *Honey, Vance said that he's not too far away, but he wants you to try and get out of the building. Then you're to tell me where you are.*

I'm not sure just yet. I...Vance saved me. He said that he knew that and was going to thank him every day for the rest of his life. *I'm still in the building. I'm working my way around the place. I can hear voices, and I think I should avoid just popping out in front of them.*

Vance told me that you were in the business district, but not much else. I think he thought that I'd get hurt or worse if we let the bad guys know that you're safe. Or that I might mess up his plans. I'm sort of not sane where you're concerned. She told him that she loved him. *And I love you as well. When I get you, don't even think that you're going to rest up or anything like that. I'm taking you to the bedroom and fucking you until you can't leave me again.*

I didn't actually leave you this time. When the voices moved away, she started walking again. Her hand was throbbing a little and she thought that she was dripping a blood trail behind her. Wrapping her hand up in her shirt, she told Jorden about it. *I can't really see it yet, but it hurts. He told me to be careful, that it was sharp, and in my haste to get free, I didn't heed his advice.*

When I come and get you, we'll go see Kenton. He can stitch it up if he needs to, and make sure that there is no infection. She leaned against the wall again when she felt tears fill her eyes. *Honey, it's going to be all right. As soon as you're safely out of the building, I'm coming to get you.*

Gavin, is he all right? Jorden told her he was with him and worried, but fine. *My grandma has no marker, and I've not been able to go and see her yet. My whole life has changed, some of it good, some of it bad, because I picked up a junk box at an auction and tried on a pair of pretty earrings. Jorden, will it be any better for the other women when they find their pieces?*

I don't know. I think.... I would think not. I know that's not what you want to hear, but there are a lot of people out there, I guess, who want a part of this. She asked him what it was that they might get. *The power to control the dragon.* She told him that was just too scary to think about right now.

She moved to the doorway that was under the most windows. She had no idea why she thought it was going to be crowded when she got out of this place, but that was her plan. To get out, blend in enough so that she could get somewhere

125

safe until Jorden came for her. But when she opened the door, she could only stare.

Large empty buildings surrounded her. Some of the windows were boarded up, and those that weren't were broken. There were signs in front of a few of them. A carpet warehouse. Another was called Morton's Hardware. A few of the buildings had even been painted on, so long ago now that the lettering was faded, but no less beautiful in the art of it. She wondered what it had been like in its heyday. How many people had simply walked the sidewalk looking for a great deal or someone to sell them carpet. To take her mind off the fear and pain she was in, she talked to Jorden.

Do you or any of your family own buildings here in the business district? Because I have to tell you, to call it that is really giving the wrong impression. He asked her what she meant. *Well, for starters, there is no business at all. Not a single one. And most of the buildings look like they've been empty longer than I've been around. How can anyone not care for a part of their history like this?*

I don't know, love. I think I might own one of them. It was part of a deal that the family took on about ten years ago. Kenton does as well, but I don't know who else. Why? What did you have in mind? She told him nothing as yet, but it seemed a shame. *Once you get back here in my arms and we're sated, if that is ever going to happen, we'll talk about the empty buildings.*

If we talk about them now, I won't have to think about how terrified I am and how much my hand hurts. She looked down at her blood stained shirt. *It's really bleeding. I might have cut myself deeper than I thought.*

Don't look at it. Look at the street names. I'm pulling up my information now. He sounded scared, which didn't help her. *Okay, there are two that I own there. One is on Market Street. And the other is on.... Let me look here. Okay, the other is on Winder. No street or avenue, just Winder. The paperwork that I have on the first one says that it used to be a factory, but not of what. The second one was at one time a place that made bricks. Cobblestones, I guess.*

She looked at the street sign she was under, but she was distracted by the building that was to her left. Jasmine fell in love with the old building and asked him what the address was of the building he owned. When he told her, she nearly wept with joy.

It's Winder Avenue, and the building is beautiful. I think at one time it was a bakery too. There are signs for bread painted on it from about the thirties, I think. He told her that it was a local bakery called, of all things, Winder Bakery. *That's about right. I want to put a shop in here when you get things squared away.*

Anything you want, love. I'll even buy up the other buildings too. But you have to come to me. I can't get there until you tell me it's safe. Vance is afraid that if I show myself there, it will mess up his plans to catch them. She wasn't entirely sure why it had to be that way, but she made her way around the building and to where she could hear cars and other business sounds. *Where are you now?*

I can see a shop called Second Hand in front of me. He told her that she was perhaps a block or so from Kenton's offices. *Should I go there?*

Yes, but please be careful. While you're around people, we don't know who is looking for you. She asked him why he'd not been able to come and get her. *Because our house is being watched, and Vance said that we didn't want anyone to know that you're safe just yet. He said that if I were to leave and they follow me to where you were, then they'd know that we're on to them.*

He told me that he was trying to get more information on another piece. He said that he needs to make sure that whoever the woman is, that she is safe too. Jorden said that is what he'd told him as

well. *I can see Kenton's office. I'm at the back where the parking....
He is at the door waving for me to come to him.*

Be careful, love. And I'll be there soon. She told him she'd be
all right now and started for the door. *Kenton said that he can
see you, and you have no idea how good that makes me feel. Just sit,
Gavin and I are on our way.*

Those were the best words she'd heard in all of her life.
As soon as she entered the back door, Kenton grabbed her up
in his arms and hugged her. It felt wonderful, but she started
crying and jabbering about pain and bakeries. He must have
understood because in no time, he had her in an office and
was cleaning her wounds. She had cut herself worse than
she'd thought.

Chapter 9

Gavin watched as Uncle Kenton put the stitches in his mom's hand and wrist. She was getting fluids pumped into her as well. Uncle Kenton had told them that she'd lost a bit of blood, but he also wanted to flush out her system in the event they'd given her more than chloroform to knock her out. He held her hand in his and talked about what he'd done while she'd been gone.

"I got all the stuff in my room tagged. Dad said that I could get rid of whatever I wanted, but that you got first dibs. He also said that if you sold them for me that I could have the money, minus your cut, and use it how I want. I'm going to open a savings account so I can have money to buy a house. Or a car. I haven't decided which yet. I might need a car before I need a house." His mom said his name. "Yeah, I'm going a mile a minute, but you have no idea how terrified I was when they told me you'd been taken."

"I'm okay now." He nodded but wasn't so sure. Uncle Kenton said that one of the cuts was really bad. "He's going to make sure I'm all right before he lets me leave here, you know

129

that, don't you?"

"Yes. But when Grannie went to bed that night, she told me she was all right too." Tears filled his eyes when he thought of losing his mom. "Please don't die on me, Mom. I love you, and you're my mom."

"I love you too, baby. But ask Kenton. He'll tell you I'm going to be all right." Kenton nodded as he worked. "See. I know it looks bad, but really, we're all going to be fine once the bad guys are gone."

"And we're working on that part too." Gavin didn't point out to Uncle Kenton that there were more than just the ones they knew about right now. He'd heard Vance and Dad talking about the long list of idiots that were trying to get the jewelry. "Also, you're going to have protection all the time now, as is Emma. And Vance is going to give us some really good news, hopefully today, on what is going on with the idiot that took your mom today."

Gavin knew they were doing the best that they could, but he wasn't sure it was going to be enough. These guys wanted her, and they didn't seem to be stopping at getting what they wanted. He touched the earring on her ear that was closest to him.

"I'm so sorry." She asked him for what. "I told you to put them in. I talked you into it that night, and since then, everything has gone badly for us. I'm not saying that Grannie dying was my fault, she was really sick, but—"

"You stop right there. I put them in, and the last time I looked, I was an adult. I don't always make sound decisions, I'm not perfect, but putting these into my ears was my decision, not anyone else's. Also, you have to think of things this way, Gavin. Had I not put them in, do you think it would have stopped those men from coming after us? Or that even after I gave them up, that they would have said thanks and left it at that?" He shook his head. "No, they wouldn't have. And by me putting them in that night, not only did it get us the best help we could get in keeping us safe, but it gave us Jorden and the rest of the McCades too."

"But they're in danger too." She shook her head at him and he nodded. "Yes they are. Those men are coming here, and we led them right to them."

"They were already here." Gavin looked at Uncle Kenton. "Emma had men following her well before she met up with us. Had she not broken into this very office and tried to get herself help, those men would have killed her and I would never have known the greatest love of my life. You two being here is no different. We'll gather our wagons around each other, and the other women that come here, and pray for the best, and kick their asses all over the place when they get uppity with us. It's the best we can do. But this is in no way, shape, or form your fault, Gavin. We were dragons long before you and your little family joined us. In fact, you being here has made us stronger."

"I want you all to be safe. I don't want my mom hurt, or any of you guys either. I love you all." Uncle Kenton assured him that he wanted that as well, and that they all loved him too. "My mom, she's all I have, and I can't be without her."

"I understand. I don't know what I'd do without my mom around. I hate to think about losing her too. But we're your family now, Gavin. And will be for the rest of our lives. You should also know that when the bad guys come again, we're going to be more than ready for them. You'll see." Gavin nodded but said nothing. When Uncle Kenton lifted his chin up and had him look at him, Gavin wanted to cry like a little kid. "My mom, she's the sweetest, kindest person I know. But

131

when my dad came to her home once and tried to hurt Lewis by holding him down and trying to cut his head off with an ax, my mom pulled out a gun and shot him twice in the head. Just like that, she ended the problem."

"She killed a man?" Uncle Kenton nodded and smiled. "I love her to pieces, but now I might be afraid of her just a little. She really killed a man? Aren't you just a little afraid of her knowing that?"

"I am. A lot. But I also love her as much as she loves me. And I know that she'd never do anything to hurt any of us." He laughed. "But don't tell her that. I don't want her to use it against me when I know a secret. Like what we're getting her for her birthday or something."

Gavin felt better; not great, but better. When his mom dozed off again, he just watched her sleep. He wanted to never leave her side again, but that was as unpractical as it could get.

When Uncle Kenton said he was finished, Dad came into the room. He'd been told he had to go if he couldn't contain himself. Apparently, he was a little nuts when it came to blood and those he loved. Jorden smiled at him and took Mom's other hand when Uncle Kenton left them alone.

"Having her hurt makes me a little on edge. I would imagine that I'd be the same way with you getting hurt." Gavin said nothing, his heart aching too badly at the moment. "Son, she's going to be all right from this. A little tired because of the drug they used, and she'll have to not use her hand a bit, but she's fine."

"I don't want her hurt." Dad said that he didn't either. As they sat there, neither of them saying anything, Gavin thought of all the things that could have gone wrong today. And when Dad said his name again, he looked at him.

"I can see the worry on you. Smell it as well." Gavin nodded. "I'm going to tell you something. It's all true, so I want you to believe me when I tell you that things have a way of working out no matter how bad it looks at the beginning."

"Uncle Kenton told me that Grandma killed her husband when he tried to hurt Uncle Lewis." Dad said she had, but that wasn't it. "You mean she really did it?"

"Yes. And she was beaten up pretty badly by then too. My dad, he wasn't a nice person, nor was he a very tolerant person. Most of the time he'd come home only to beat the crap out of Mom and take whatever money was around the house." Dad shivered as if he was remembering something else. "But that's not what I wanted to tell you. When I was nine or so, Kenton and I were playing in the backyard. It wasn't that big of a deal for us to be out of Mom's sight for hours on end. Vance was out there as well, but he was doing his own thing. Much like he does now. Anyway, as we were getting our crap gathered up that only little boys can find, we saw this streak of black run by us."

"Wolf?" Dad said no, it was a bear. "There are bears around here too? Do you think you can introduce them to me?"

"I will with the ones that I know, but this was a wild bear. And he was hurt." Gavin knew that animals when hurt or cornered could be a little nutty, but Dad continued before he could ask which he was. "He had rabies and he wasn't right in his head. While we were trying to figure out what to do, where to go and not have him run us down, a large man came out of nowhere and hit him with a ball bat. Now I know what you're thinking; what would make a grown man hit a bear with a bat? And I have to tell you, Kenton and I thought the same thing. But before the man could hit him again, the bear turned on him and the man told us to run when he did."

Gavin held his mom's hand just a little tighter as Dad got up to pace the room. When he finally sat down again, Gavin wasn't sure if he wanted him to continue or to stop right where he was.

"The man was hit in the back by the bear, knocking him head over ass into the creek we'd been playing by. Vance was down there too, and when he came up to see what was going on, the bear spotted him." Dad looked at him then. "When he took off toward Vance, no doubt to kill him, the man threw the bat toward Kenton and I. Now remember, we were just kids. But this bear was going to hurt our brother, so when Kenton picked it up, I found myself a rock and hit the bear with it."

"Did he turn to you then?" Dad nodded, his face grim. "What did you do? I mean, a bat and a few rocks isn't much to fight a grown bear."

"No, it wasn't, but when he came at us again, Kenton put the bat on his shoulder like he was ready for a grand slam. The faster he came at us, getting closer all the time, I knew we were going to die. Both of us would be nothing but a gut mess, I remember thinking, and then he'd go after Vance and the man who had tried to save us." Dad looked out the little window in the room as he told the rest of the story. "He was nearly atop us by then, just a few feet separated us from him, when he just dropped to his knees, then onto his belly. It took us a few seconds to realize that he was dead. When Kenton dropped to his knees as well, I thought for sure he'd been hurt, but he said he was fine, just scared to death."

"The man had a gun." Dad nodded. "And he shot him so that you'd be all right. Why didn't he just use the gun in the first place?"

"He said he'd been afraid of hitting one of us. But he

didn't kill the bear, Gavin. Vance did it. He pulled the man's gun out of his pants and shot the bear once in the head, killing him immediately." Gavin sat there in stunned silence. "So you see, even when things look really bad, and it really did for us, something or someone will come through and help you. And Vance? He's still saving our asses all the time."

"I'm surely glad that he's on our side." Dad said he was as well. "I don't know if I wouldn't have wet myself with a bear coming at me."

"Let me tell you something that I've never told another soul. I was nearly at that point myself when it turned on us." Gavin nodded. "We're going to be all right, Gavin. I swear this to you."

Gavin believed him too. His dad had helped fell a bear and had come out on top. And even with a rock, he was going to help protect his family. Gavin felt like him and his mom were in good hands with the McCade family. He almost felt sorry for the bad guys.

~~~

Richard wasn't sure what was going on, but the woman was gone. And his brother was royally pissed off at him. When he shone his flashlight again over the area that she'd been at when he'd left not two hours ago, he saw the blood, but no woman. She'd been tied up, so whoever helped her out was going to pay for making him look bad.

"She's gone and hurt herself." Wilburn just stared at him. Like he was waiting for him to just keel over and die. "I thought if we had her and the earrings you'd feel better about stuff. That you'd not be so angry at me all the time. I wanted to give her to you as a gift."

Not really. What he'd wanted to do was to bring his brother here with Vance and have him kill his brother. He figured that since he'd already told Vance that Wilburn had taken her, it would be nothing for the man to shoot Wilburn between the eyes. But Vance, like he did to him all the time, hadn't shown up. Not returned his dozen or so calls either. They were going to have to talk about this, Richard thought.

"And how did you expect me to feel better about *stuff*, Richard? Because the McCades surely know by now that you kidnapped one of their own." Richard didn't point out that they thought Wilburn had done the kidnapping, but told him again that he was sorry she'd gotten away. "So am I. So am I. I can hear it all now, McCade Broad Brings Down the Glass Men."

"Do you really think they'd call her a broad?" Wilburn growled at him. "Well, that's what you said, you know. And how was I supposed to know that she'd get free? I had her all tied up around her arms and legs. Do you think she might have had some kind of weapon on her? I never thought to check on that."

"Of course you didn't. That is why you're in deep shit over this, and I'm going to let you wallow in it." Richard said nothing, knowing that he'd already talked to Vance and told him his version of what had happened. "What is it you supposed was going to happen here? That she'd just lay there and let us cut her up, and then we'd let her go afterwards? I'm curious how you had this whole plot worked out in your head."

"I just wanted to be helpful." To get Wilburn dead and out of his way in this. But he didn't voice the last part. He was pretty sure that his brother would kill him if he did. "What would you have done differently? If you're so perfect, what would you have done?"

"I would have drugged her, cut the fucking earrings off,

136

and then killed her where she stood. No fucking around. No taking her somewhere so she could be found. Or in your case, where she could fucking get away and tell on me." Richard thought he did have a point. But Wilburn's way would have gotten nothing for Richard. His way, the best way, was where Wilburn would have been arrested, tried, and sent to prison, if not killed by Richard's partner. Richard would have it all then. Even the earrings and whatever else might come with them. "Are you working out what you're going to say to the police when they find you? Because I'm not going to lift a fucking finger to help you out of this mess. You did it, you suffer through it."

"You never did think I was very smart." Wilburn said nothing, but Richard could tell that he was agreeing with him. "You really don't think there is a dragon, do you? And that he's going to come to you when you call him? Seriously, there are no such things as dragons. Everyone in their right mind knows that."

The sound in the other part of the building had them both drawing their guns. There were men out there, six with Wilburn and two with him. It occurred to Richard then that his brother always had the best. The best men, the best toys when they were children. He wanted to kill him now, just take it all, but the noise had him afraid and Richard decided that he might need Wilburn for a little while longer.

"Who is it?" Richard said he had no idea. "Did you think that the woman could find her way back here, and has even now led the police to us? Christ, that's all I need. To be at the scene of the crime I had no part in, but it will be thought that I have. Richard, you fucking bastard, you've fucked us both over this time."

"Be quiet. I think they can hear us. Do you want to be

killed too?" Wilburn pointed the gun at his head and Richard knew he was going to pull the trigger this time. "What if they hear you?"

"Right now I think I'd gladly go to jail for killing you." The noise sounded again and Richard backed up against the wall, out from in front of the doorway. The short scream had him thinking that their men were being attacked, but that wasn't possible. No one had fired a single bullet as yet.

"What do you suppose is going on?"

Wilburn shrugged but said nothing more. Richard was afraid that it might be Vance. That man scared him enough to have his bowels act up and his sphincter muscle tighten up so badly that he couldn't take a good crap for a few days after feeling his anger released. When he opened his mouth to ask his brother if he was going to save them, Wilburn looked at him.

"Will you shut the fuck up so I can think?" Nodding, he waited on his brother while he thought them out of this mess. Whoever was out there, they weren't going to get past Wilburn. He was a good shot and had a lot of men at his beck and call. When the noise startled them both again, Richard thought about all the things he'd not been able to do because he'd been so broke all the time.

"I need some more money." Wilburn asked him what he was talking about. "Money. I want you to give me more. I don't have nearly as much as you do, and Mom and Dad left it to us both."

"In the event that it has somehow slipped your mind, we're about to be murdered where we stand. For fuck sake, Richard, your timing, as usual, is impeccable." Richard didn't think any time was a good time to talk to his brother about money. "When we get out of this, or if, I will talk to you about money. Right now, if it's all the same to you, I'd like to not end up in prison with you as a cell mate. Or worse yet, on a slab in a morgue shot to fuck because you're an idiot."

The noise stopped after that. There wasn't anyone coming in the door, and Richard had a feeling that the men out there had been playing a mean joke on them. When the door to the room they were in suddenly opened, Richard lifted his gun and fired five times — bang, bang, bang, bang, bang — into the person standing there. It wasn't until he shone his flashlight over the body that he realized his mistake.

"Mother fuck." He looked at his brother when he started cursing. "You just fucking killed one of my best men. What do you plan to do now, dance a little jig with your dick flapping in the wind? You moronic fuck."

"He just came out of nowhere." Richard waited while his brother checked the man's pulse. He was pretty sure that the man was dead. There were two bullet holes in his head and three in his chest. It would take a miracle for him to have survived that. When Wilburn stood up, he asked about his health.

"I think he might pull through. I mean, he's lost nearly all his blood and his brain is laying under his head, but he might just pull through." There was a tone that didn't sound like he was telling him the truth. "He's dead. What did you expect to happen when you plugged him full of more holes than I have ties in my closet?" Richard said he only shot him a couple of times. "You shot him five fucking times. And now he's dead, and you're the one who killed him."

Richard moved out into the room and saw the men they had come with standing there as if nothing had happened and he'd not just killed one of their own. They asked Wilburn if he was all right. He said he was, then asked them what all that noise had been, and Richard thought he was going to blame it on one of them.

"There was a homeless guy trying to set himself up. We ran him off, and Ben was going to tell you guys in case you heard him." No one asked, and Richard wondered if they had cared about the guy at all. "Do you want us to take care of this?"

"No. I want you to fucking leave him here to be found so my dumbassed brother goes to jail." When the men just stood there, Richard was sure that was what was going to happen. "Get this cleaned up and take care that no one knows anything."

When they had taken the body away, Richard tried to think how he could make this his brother's fault. It wouldn't be hard, he supposed. He had Vance eating out of the palm of his hand. And the man believed everything he told him, too. When they were headed out to the car that had brought them here, Richard asked Wilburn if he wanted to get some dinner.

"Dinner? With you? No. I think not. I've had about all of you I can take for one day. As a matter of fact, I want you to stop coming around all together. I can't do this with you anymore." Richard laughed and said they were brothers. "Yes. The only reason that you're not dead yet is for that one reason. Stay away from me, Richard. I've got enough going on right now without you fucking things up."

"What about the McCades and all that shit going on?" Wilburn asked him what he thought he had to contribute to things. "Well, I have the bugs that I'm working on. Then there is my in with the McCades. I can get you intel that no one else can."

"Yes, you have a bug in an office that I have had bugged for weeks. You also said you were going to go to the police department and bug that office. Did you do that?" Richard said he'd done it just that day. "Good. That's good. But let me ask you something, Richard. Did you perhaps wear gloves when you planted said bugs? Or even the one in the artist's building? Did you take precautions so that you'd not get caught if they found them?"

"Gloves?" His brother rocked on his heels several times and smiled at him. There was something about him that just irritated him to no end. "Why would I wear gloves, Wilburn? It's summer time. I think there might be something wrong—"

"Fingerprints, you moron. Don't you read the paper? Perhaps watch the news, or even one of those shows that they're forever showing where the bad men were caught by simply not taking any precautions in their trying to get ahead?" Richard thought that perhaps he'd gladly kill his only brother right now. With a smile on his face. "You are far and away the dumbest man I have ever had the misfortune of being related to."

"Well, don't you think that's a little harsh?" Richard looked around the area and then back at his brother. "No, I did not use gloves. It never occurred to me as I work with Vance. Whatever happens, if they happen to find the bugs, will not have any effect on me simply because he and I are working together. I don't know what I'll tell him about the prints, but he'll believe me. I do think him to be slightly stupid."

"You do, do you? Well, again, you're wrong about this. I had someone look into his life. Did you know that he is one of the most elite men in the world? Not the state of Ohio, but the entire fucking world. Not only have he and his men done more work before most people get out of their beds, but it is rumored that at some point in his career with the United States Special Forces he has killed more men than you can line up

141

foot to head to go across the US. Fuck, Richard, he could kill you with only his finger should he want to." Richard laughed. There wasn't any way this man had done any such thing, and he told his brother that. "Your funeral. But I'm done with you. As of today, we're no longer related."

As Wilburn walked away from him, Richard asked him again if he wanted to get some dinner. He wasn't surprised when he flipped him off. Wilburn was such an asshole. But he loved him, and knew that he was only kidding.

CHAPTER 10

Jorden felt his body come to life. Not only was he as hard as stone, but his beautiful mate was atop him, taking her own pleasure. Naked. And the most beautiful vision he'd ever had the pleasure of witnessing. When she looked down at him and smiled, he held onto her hips to slow her down, just until he caught up, he told himself.

"You were so hard all I could think about was riding you." He nodded and moaned when she leaned over him and took his nipple into her mouth and bit him. "You taste good too, but when I had you in my mouth, all I wanted to do was feel you like this. I hope you don't mind. I needed you."

"You can wake me this way anytime you wish." He rolled his hips up to meet each of her downwards thrusts. "Christ, you're beautiful. And all mine. Ride me, baby."

"Make me come, Jorden. I want to come on you this way." He sat up and pulled her breast into his mouth. As he suckled hard on just the tip, she wrapped her arms around his head and held him to her. "I'm so close. I can feel it all over me, the need to come. Help me, please?"

"When you come, I'm going to roll you over to your back and fuck you hard." Her movements became erratic, her breath, hot against his face, was a pant now. Taking her breast into his mouth again, he sucked more into his mouth. Sliding his hand between her legs, feeling how wet and hard her nubbin was, Jorden bit down hard on her breast and tasted her blood. And when he did, he pinched her clit at the same time, knowing that she was going to explode.

Her scream was loud, as if she had been holding it within her for days and perhaps months. When she came a second, then a third time, he rolled her to her back and pounded her as hard as he could. Her hands were touching him, tugging at him, as if to bring him closer, tighter to her body.

Wrapping her legs around him, Jorden lifted her ass up, bringing her as tight to him as he could and still be able to fuck her. When she cried out she was coming again, her body bowed up off the bed, nearly unseating him. As his own body prepared to empty into hers, his balls close to his body aching with need, Jorden bit down on her throat, tasting her blood as he emptied himself into her.

Again. His dragon screamed at him that he wasn't finished, wasn't nearly done marking his mate. Jorden felt his body fill, his cock harden more, and when he came this time, his body burning with the need to claim her, he felt his dragon slip from him, taking his body for just a second as he bit Jasmine. Coming this time, he knew something was different, something more had come from the dragon.

Her scream was different too, full of pain this time. Jorden begged the dragon to release her, to let her go. But before he could convince him that he was indeed hurting their mate, he came, his body emptying once again deep inside of her.

Then just as quickly as he'd taken him, the dragon released

him. Jorden dropped onto Jasmine, not just from not having the strength to do anything more, but he was sure that he could easily pass out. Rolling to his back took all that he had. It was then that he realized that Jasmine was sobbing. That he had truly hurt her.

"I'm so sorry, love. I don't know what happened just then." She held him to her, her body shaking she was crying so hard. Jorden felt his own tears fill his eyes. He hurt too; he'd hurt his mate, and it tore at him. "I love you, Jasmine. I don't know what came over me. Dragon said I needed…I'm not going to blame him. It was all me. I'm so terribly sorry I hurt you."

She is with child, my lord. Jorden asked the dragon—Caelin, Jasmine had told him his name was—what he meant. *Your dragon, he knew that she is…I know not the word. Ripe? Her body received your seed and now she is with child. You're to be a father and her a mother again.*

"No, that's not possible." Jasmine lifted her tear stained face and he wiped at it, telling her what Caelin had said. "He said that my dragon, he knew that you were ovulating and that he.... Well, I gave you a child."

"A baby?" She rolled to her back, leaving him lying there to look down at her. "We're going to have a baby? You and I? Is he sure about this?"

"You don't sound upset about it." She grinned at him. "Okay, I'm going to take that as you're thrilled to death with having a child. So now what do we do?"

"Are you?" He put his hand on her flat belly and thought of a child growing there, his child. "I mean, it's a little late for that now, I guess. But we never really talked about children. And there is Gavin to consider. I told him we'd talk about this before we made this sort of…I'm really going to have a baby?

Your baby?"

Yes, you're going to have a child. You will have a dragon child in several months, and she will be stronger than any born before her. I know not how long it takes, but your child, I can feel her there now, she will be more dragon than not, and she will have all that you have. More, should the pieces of myself come together. Which I do believe...yes, I believe that you will be able to do this. Bring the dragons in all of you to life. Jorden thought of a child, a dragon child of his being born, and his heartrate tripled. He was going to have a child. *You are happy, my lord?*

"Gavin will have to know immediately. And we'll...I don't think I want to tell anyone else right now." Jorden agreed. The longer they had to hold this secret to them, he thought it would be better. Not that they all wouldn't be thrilled to death, but Christ...they were going to have another child. "Are you happy?"

"Yes. Terrified, but happy." She nodded, but he could see that he'd taken some of her joy away. "I won't lie to you; I have all these thoughts going through my head right now that you're going to think are strange."

"Like what? And so you know, I understand being afraid. And even though I have done this before, I'm no less frightened of what can happen. What things can go wrong." He nodded and told her that was what was in his head too. "I understand, but I think we're going to be just fine. Tell me what you're thinking, Jorden."

"I don't know how to be a father. I mean, I'm so worried every time that Gavin comes to me that I'm going to give him bad advice or not know the answer to something." Jorden laughed. "Okay, he is a hell of a lot smarter than me so doesn't really come to me with questions, but I want to be a good father to him. Someone he can lean on and respect. I was feeling like

I might not fuck him up too badly, and now we're going to have another child I might mess up. I haven't any idea about schools or colleges for either of them. What if she hates me?"

"Oh, Jorden. No one could ever hate you. You're a good man and a great father. Gavin is already calling you Dad and looking up to you. And he's just as afraid as you are about being a son." Jorden asked her how that was possible. "He's never had a very good father relationship. His dad, while around a little, was never there for him. All he could do was bemoan the fact that he was dirt poor and his lover had left him. Kris never took him to ball games, asked about his homework or how he was doing in school. I've heard you ask him all kinds of things about his day. And you and the others have that plan to go to the first football game of the season. Gavin is thrilled to death about that."

They stood up and Jasmine got dressed. Jorden continued to voice his concerns and Jasmine, while she didn't shoot them down, sometimes laughed at his fears. They were pretty silly, he supposed. What did it matter now if she got a diaper rash? Or if she wanted her room to be blue or pink? She'd be happy, Jasmine told him, and that was all that mattered.

Jorden thought of Gavin while he was showering. And then when he was dressed and headed to the kitchen, all he could think about was his son might not be happy about the baby. Jorden was, or he was getting there. He wasn't unhappy about the baby, just overwhelmed, he supposed. He had no idea how to care for an infant…or how to change a diaper, nor did he have the slightest clue what to do when they cried.

When he entered the kitchen, he saw Gavin eating his breakfast and Jorden sat down with him. "We're having a baby." The spoon dropped into his bowl as Gavin stared at him. "I guess we're having a girl. Caelin told us it was a girl. And she'll be dragon too. I don't know how to change a diaper. Do you?"

"No. But I'm sure we can learn. Do you think that's going to be a problem? And you sound a little freaked out." Jorden nodded and tried to think beyond all the million and one questions that were hopping around in his head like the Easter Bunny on Easter morning. "Are you all right?"

"I have no idea. I thought, you know, that it'd be a while. Build up to me learning how to be a dad and so on. The diaper part is just the tip of the iceberg, I think." Jorden looked at Gavin. "I want you to know that I'm thrilled about this, but I want you to be as well."

"I love the idea about having a little sister. And I think you're doing a great job at being my dad." Jorden nodded. "All the stuff that is running in your head right now can be learned. I'm pretty sure that Grandma will gladly help us learn how to put a diaper on her."

"She'll be happy too. Two grandchildren. She'll think she's the queen of all grandmothers." Gavin said he thought she was. "Good for you. But I have to tell you, I'm sick with worry about your mom. We'll have to make sure she doesn't overdo things and that she eats right."

"Yeah? Well, if it's all the same to you, I'm not going to tell my mom she needs a nap or that she needs more leafy green stuff." They both laughed and Jorden felt better for it. "You don't look as freaked out now. Are we really having a baby? A sister for me?"

"Yes. And I'm not *as* freaked out, as you called it. I mean, I'm still thinking of all the things that could hurt her and the baby, but it's not so overwhelming." Gavin picked up his spoon and phone. When he found whatever he'd been looking for he handed it to him. "What's this?"

"How to change a diaper for dummies. I think we need to find more videos like this one." As he watched it, the woman doing it slowly so that he could see each step, Jorden didn't think it was so bad. "We'll need all kinds of stuff for her too, I guess. Do you know what you're going to name her yet? And then there is furniture. I don't think I saw a nursery in this place."

"No, I don't think there is one either. But we're waiting a bit before—" The next diaper was a poopie one. That was what she called it, a poopie diaper. Jorden felt his belly lurch up when she lifted the baby's bottom up off the dark stain and began wiping it with some sort of smallish cloth. "Christ, I can't do this. Here, watch this."

By the time Jasmine joined them in the kitchen, they had watched six more videos, as well as looked up how to bathe a baby and what was the best formula that should be used. Gavin was making notes, Abby was making fun of them, and Jorden needed air. He decided that he wasn't going to make a good father after all.

"You two need to take a time out." Jasmine looked at the current video and grinned at him. "Have you watched the one where the baby poops in the bath water and the father is covered in it? I mean, it's in his hair, his fingers. I think he even had some on his mouth."

Jorden stood up and left the kitchen. They were laughing when he sat on the deck, but he didn't care. He was never changing a diaper so long as he lived. Especially not one that was filled with poop. What kind of name was poop anyway? When Jasmine joined him on the deck, he took her hand in his. It was time for him to confess he wasn't going to be any help to her.

"You're going to help me and love it." He shook his head.

"Yes you will. I promise. And after a couple of days, you'll not even care that she has a load in her diaper when she falls asleep in your arms. Or takes your finger into her little hand. You'll look down at her while you're giving her a bottle and think, I created something right here and it's a part of me. All the stuff that is running in your head that could go wrong? Yeah, it could. And tomorrow I could get hit by a bus. But you have to enjoy the things you have while you have them. I'm not saying that I won't mess up. I will, but—"

"I'll fuck up." She said that she was sure every parent did. But they learned from their mistakes. "What if she hates me? I mean, Gavin is old enough that if I screw up too badly, I know he can fix it. But this baby is going to be depending on me to keep her safe and out of harm. I couldn't even save you from being kidnapped by those bastards."

"You never let me give up on myself, Jorden. And even though I walked out of that building on my own, you were there with me every step of the way. It'll be the same for our children. You be there, guide them, and hope that when they're away from the house, they remember that you love them more than anything in this world. The best way that you know how." He wasn't so sure and said that to her. "You will. And do me a favor, no more videos. You and Gavin can ask questions if you want to know something. Borrow someone's baby for an hour, but no more watching people care for or make fun of their children. You'll be fine."

~~~

Jasmine moved along the aisle of furniture and tried to think how the hell she was going to make this work. There was just too much of it. Everywhere she stepped, there was something that needed to be moved or placed. When she'd gone through the things at the other place, she'd had it spread out. Now they'd just brought it in and dropped it right in the middle of everything. When she looked at Aisha when she said her name, she both wanted to run and hide and cry at the same time.

"Take a deep breath and let it out slowly." Nodding, she did just what she was told. "Now, think about what you want, where you want something, and we'll work on getting it taken care of. You've never met Ralph Donavan, have you? Well, he's the pack alpha to the wolves that roam our land. He has sent over some of his men to help us get this organized. And Kenton dropped off the carts you asked for, so when you're ready, we're ready."

"The only way we can get organized is if we start over. I should have been thinking about how many pieces there were and what I was going to do with them." Aisha pointed out that she'd only had a few days. "In the event you can't tell, I'm slightly overwhelmed."

"Well of course you are. Come now, we can do this. How about you think where you want this piece here? By the way, I love this. I have no idea what its primary use is, but I like it. Just forget that there are a lot of pieces and focus on them one at a time." Jasmine nodded and looked at the tall boy in front of her. Just looking at the piece, she felt a little calmness settle over her.

"It's called a tall boy. See, it has drawers here and a wardrobe on top. Not to be confused with a highboy, which has a double, sometimes triple, set of drawers in one space. I think it has more pieces to it." Jasmine pulled out her inventory sheet to look at the number she'd assigned it. "Yes. There is a smaller dresser, a headboard, as well as one nightstand. There were two, but the other one isn't in good shape." Two men came up with a large dolly and she told them to find the other

151

pieces that had the same number and put them against the south wall. "This piece has two others that match it. We'll put them in the same area. Sort of a bedroom furniture section."

After that, things went better. And when she had an entire area filled with all the bedroom sets she had, Jasmine put some of the single items along with it just to fill out the area. There were boxes of decorations things too that she set in the area, lamps that would be set up to bring light to the area, and little knickknacks that were the biggest money maker to her when she'd flip things. And Jasmine had found boxes and boxes of doilies that she wanted to display and sell too.

The second floor had the kitchen department. There were a lot of single chairs...a few sets, but not many. And when she had a table brought up, a pretty oak that had three leaves that went with it, she put some of the oak chairs around it, making sure that none of them matched. The three sideboards were put against the wall, with several boxes of glass and pottery items set on them to be displayed later. There were also several pie safes, all in great shape, as well as cupboards that were used to make pies on. Two even had their flour sifter still intact. Those pieces alone were going to be a showstopper, she thought to herself.

As soon as Jorden and Lewis showed up with two new mattress and box spring sets, she sent them to help her make up the beds. She'd found several old quilts, as well as some gorgeous hand stitched pillow cases and sheet sets with the boxes of things that she'd gotten, and was happy to see how nice they looked on the bed. Going to the kitchen area again when Dalton came with sandwiches and drinks, Jasmine was happy to see that Aisha and Gavin had started laying out the dinner sets, as well as some of the older kitchen items.

"Do you have use for a jewelry case?" She asked Grady

if he had one. "I do. There are a lot of things like that at my house. There are also a lot of jewelry pieces still in it that Emma didn't want. I got one of her father's homes when he passed away, and all the contents. If you want them, I have a lot of stuff that I have no use for. Some of them better than the things you have in here."

"I don't know a lot about jewelry. Furniture is more what I know, as well as some glass. I had books, a lot of them, at my old home. They're gone now, but I guess we could look them up." Gavin laughed. "You're going to tell me that I have the Internet again and that I can just look things up that way, aren't you? Well, I like looking things up in books. It's more…I don't know, I guess personal for me."

"You have books here." They all turned to Lewis when he spoke. "I saw them. I mean, there are a lot of them too. I moved them to the little area you said you were going to use for an office."

As she followed him into the back room, all she could think about was how much Grannie would have loved this. But as soon as she entered the back room, all she could do was stare at it. It didn't look this way a few days ago.

"We wanted to give you a business warming gift." Jorden was sitting at the desk she had been wanting since she found it in the other building. It had been old and stained, the dust on it too thick to even tell what wood it had been. Now it was shiny, the brass fittings on the front like they were new. Tears filled her eyes when she touched her fingers to the top of it. "Gavin was very helpful in what you might need, and whatever we couldn't think of, we just had fun. Do you like it?"

There was a nice computer on the desk that had her name sliding over the screen, as well as a printer that was already loaded with paper. Several shelves were loaded with books on everything from pottery to toys. There was stock too. Boxes of tissue paper, bags, and tags. When she moved along the back part of the room, she saw a refrigerator and a microwave, as well as a pot for tea and cups. Pulling down one of the tins of tea, she looked back at Jorden and saw that the others had crowded into the room, along with Kenton and Emma. They had done this for her, given her an office she would never have gotten on her own.

"I was to keep you out of here until Kenton was finished up delivering a baby. Oh my, you gave me such a scare a couple of times when you started back this way." Aisha smiled at her as she continued. "Honey, you should have seen us trying to get this ready for you. We had so much fun that it was a pleasure to see them working on it."

"I just don't know what to say. It's all so.... No one has ever done something so grand for me before. I feel...I love you all so much."

When Jorden came to her and held her in his arms, he whispered a question to her. But when she told him that Gavin should do it, he thought it was a great idea. Looking at her son, she only had to nod and she could see that he was proud to tell the family their news.

"Mom and Dad and I have something to tell you all. I mean, I get to tell you, but it's from all of us. Well, us anyway. We wanted to wait, but with all this it's—" Vance told him to get on with it. "Yes. Okay. We're going to have a baby girl. I'm going to have a little sister."

No one moved, and Jasmine was afraid that they were unhappy. But before she could tell them they'd fucking have to get over it, Aisha screamed. And not one of those girly kinds either. More like she was going to hurt something, it was so loud.

"You're having a baby? A little girl? Oh my, this is the best news. When? Do you know that? A little girl? You're having a little girl for me." Aisha hugged Gavin to her and then three more times before she moved to them. "I'm so happy. A little girl? Oh Gavin, we're going to have so much fun when she gets here. You and I have some major planning to do, and we have to go to the zoo to do it. What do you think? Zoo? Then perhaps.... Oh my, you're going to have so much fun with Grandma."

Everyone laughed and she turned to them, clearly embarrassed. Jorden hugged her and kissed her on the cheek before he spoke. "It's okay, Mom, we know you love us. But yes, we're having a little girl. Caelin told us this morning."

Everyone congratulated her and Jorden. Even Gavin was told how glad they were that he was going to share his sister. After a little while, when it was apparent that they were going to be helping her more after this, she put them all to work on arranging not just the furniture, but all the displays as well. By nightfall, not only were they pretty much set up the way she'd wanted, but most of the items had been priced as well. Grady had helped with making pretty display signs on the sets too.

Walking to the pizza parlor, they were still talking about what sort of name the antique place should have. Several were tossed around, but she had an idea she wanted to discuss with Gavin and Jorden first. Then there was the business district that she wanted to talk to the family about now.

"How many of the buildings does this family own? Keep in mind that there are nineteen large buildings there that are empty, and two that will be soon if they don't get some help. As well as four houses and a large restaurant that looks like it's been out of business for some time." As they counted them up, she pulled out her notepad and started writing down things she'd seen there. Jasmine had gone back to the place early this morning with Emma, and they had counted them and had ideas for the renovation of them. "Also, who owns them?"

"I own the debunked restaurant." She looked at Lewis when he spoke. "And two other buildings that I no longer remember where they are. I got them when the city was doing something to get them off their books. I think we all did."

"I think that as a whole we own all the buildings. Some of them we share with one or another of us, but for the most part, we each own a part of them." Kenton nodded at her notes as he continued. "What is it you have in your head? Because I know as well as I'm sitting here, you have a plan."

"Emma and I have a plan. And so you know, we did a quick inventory of all the buildings we could get into. A lot of them will need to be cleaned out, as in there are more than a few homeless using them. I would say kids as well, but homeless people are making use of the ones that are still intact enough to keep them warm and dry. We think, and I believe you'll agree, that in order to make this town viable again, we have to start somewhere." Lewis asked her what she wanted to do with the homeless, turn them out? "No. I think that with the help of the city, we can change a couple of the places into cheap housing for them. Maybe the houses could be used as a starting point. And barring that, a place they can get a shower as well as a decent meal."

"I like that idea." She nodded at Dalton. "Crime isn't a huge problem in that area because there is nothing there. We'd have to think about that as we move forward. Then there is the added issue of what to bring in as businesses. Because as it stands now, there is little to offer anyone even if we were to get it in better shape."

"We have a plan for that as well." Emma stood up and addressed them. Jasmine admired her a great deal, and loved her as much. "In order for us to get groceries, we have to travel to the next city over. Also, we've looked into it, and while we don't have the population to have our own post office, we can have them put in a few more boxes, as well as a place that can sell stamps and other sundries. Jasmine and I also spoke with Mom, and she thought we could have a florist, as well as a dry cleaning place. I think that Abby even mentioned that a place to have things repaired, like small appliances, would be useful as well."

"If we're making a list of things that we could use, even with the growth, we'll need a closer dentist, veterinarian, as well as a pharmacy." Grady also said that he'd like to see more kid zone places, such as old fashioned soda shops and a dairy bar. When the pizzas arrived, she had a list and also help. The men were going to contact friends to fill positions that had been mentioned. Clean up crews were talked about, as well as zoning laws that had to be looked at.

By the time they were headed to their homes, Jasmine thought that they'd made a great dent in what was needed. The town, all of it, would only benefit from all this influx of new places. And she'd make sure that it didn't fall through the cracks when the newness of it wore off.

Chapter 11

Wilburn moved to his living room and paused. Something was off. He looked around before committing himself fully to the room, but he knew that something was wrong, just not what it was. As soon as the door closed behind him and something hit him hard in the back of his head, he knew first of all it was a gun; secondly, he was in deep shit.

"Sit in the chair over there." The voice was dark, low, and male. As he made his way to the chair that he'd been directed to, the man said nothing. Wilburn wasn't sure he had any scent to him either. Not a whiff of cologne or even body smells. "We're going to have a little conversation, then I'm going to make sure that you're out of my way, you and that idiot brother of yours."

"I'm assuming you have a good reason for coming into my home uninvited." Wilburn sat down but still couldn't see the man. "What is it you think someone is going to do to me? And you should know that I have cameras all over the place... you'll be caught."

The wires fell into his lap. Not only that, but a hand drawn map did as well, and Wilburn could see that he'd gotten most of them, if not all. Dropping the stuff to the floor, Wilburn bent to pick it up and get his little gun when the man touched his own gun to his head again. Christ, this man was good. Perhaps, he thought, he'd see if he wanted to come work for him.

"Touch it and you're dead right now. And no one is coming to help you; the staff that you had is gone for the day, and all the phones are disconnected from the source. You're mine until I say differently." Wilburn sat up but said nothing. This shit was bad. Really bad. "You should also be aware that your man in California, Quincy, has been detained as well. Well, he's dead. And the two men he was with. The piece that he was sent to look at is in the hands of someone else. Not that you're going to be around to know this, but I'll have it by the end of the day tomorrow or before."

Wilburn tried to ignore the fact that he'd been told twice now that he was going to be killed. Nothing was ever settled, he thought, when he could buy his way out of it. And he would, he just had to find the man's price. Wilburn knew that everyone had a price.

"You're very informed. I'm assuming that my brother has been talking to you. And I'm betting that you're Vance McCade as well." The man only laughed. "Well, what is it you want, Vance? I'm assuming you don't mind me calling you by your first name, since you'll be going to prison soon."

"I'm not Vance. And no, I've not been talking to your brother, other than to invite him here so that he too will be out of my way. The police are going to have a time trying to figure out who killed you both. And with such precision." The light flared on and Wilburn felt his balls tighten to his body and sweat trickle down his back when he looked at the man seated

160

at his desk now. "I can see from the expression on your face that you are well aware of who I am."

"Yes. I know of you. You're Fredrick Winslow, one of the richest men in the country. Ruthless, and not without your fair share of trouble." Wilburn wondered what the fuck was going to happen now. Because the way he was seeing it, there could only be one outcome of this. He would be dead, just as the man had told him. "Is this about the pieces from the McCade ancestor?"

"Some of it. More about you and that idiot brother of yours." He leaned back in his chair and smiled at him, the gun never wavering as it was pointed at him. "You've been busy. I would have said very busy, but I don't care to give you credit when you've done nothing progressive so far. I mean, you've had the earrings nearly in your possession twice, and you've lost them. The brooch, which I'm assuming is what you thought was in California, is no longer yours. Your man there, Quincy, never stood a chance of getting it for you. Sadly, I didn't get it either, but that isn't any concern of yours, now is it?"

"Was it the one?" Winslow said nothing. "Come now, you know as well as I do that you're dying to tell me. Was it a part of the set?"

"Dying is about right. You will be soon enough. The piece? I have no idea. I have no magic to speak of, so I, like you, have no way of knowing. Your grandda, he had a little, enough to see what was right there when he saw it. However, you did not inherit it. Neither did Richard." Wilburn had heard that before. That one needed to not just be pure of heart, but also magical. He no more believed that than he did he was going to walk out of this room again. "There are two that I'm in pursuit of now. One of them is the torque."

"Torque? There is no listing for that. You're mistaken." A drawing was handed to him. He could see that someone had taken their time with it. Added in some color too, but Wilburn thought that was all it was, a drawing of a sort of bracelet that someone wanted him to believe was part of the set. "This proves nothing. My grandfather was told there were five pieces. Not six."

"You know as well as I do why there are six pieces." Wilburn had heard that as well, but it didn't make it any truer. "It matters little, really. You're never going to see them together. Nor will you be able to profit from it."

"I suppose this is your plan. To take control of one of the pieces to have the dragon at your beck and call. Good luck with that one. It's not as easy as you'd think." Winslow laughed once again and Wilburn felt his temper rise up. "What is this really all about?"

"I can tell you because, as I have said, you won't be here to see it. I plan to not have one of the pieces, but all of them. And I will not be fucking around to get them either. I see an opportunity to take one, the bearer of such a gift will never know what happened to them." He thought of his brother and his attempt to get the earrings. "Anyone wearing my pieces will simply have them cut from their body and taken. I will have them all before this is done."

"Then what? Without the women and the dragons, you know that you cannot summon him." He said nothing but smiled again. "You mean to sell them to the highest bidder, knowing that they won't work."

"They won't work with this generation of McCades, but there will be more of them. The lineage has been waiting for a time to have the pieces together forever, and one more generation will not matter to me. But I will be paid handsomely for them while they wait." Wilburn thought his plan brilliant, but said nothing. "But now I must end your life, because you have gotten in my way enough. First the ring, and then the torque and brooch." He stood up, and so did Wilburn.

"I can help you. I have a lot of contacts that can get you as much information as you want." When Winslow laughed this time, he raised up the gun so that it touched Wilburn's forehead. "Don't do this. I can help you."

Wilburn heard the laughter. It was hard and dark, like the man's voice had been. When he heard the door open to his office, he nearly cried out to be helped, but he heard Richard's voice then and knew that he'd sold him out.

"Oh good, the security code worked." It was the last sound he heard as the bullet penetrated his head.

~~~

Dalton stepped over the first body as he made his way deeper into the room. He'd been called out on double homicides before. Had even been called to a couple that had more than two bodies. But this one, these two men, had him a little nervous. He was sure that Vance had a hand in this.

No, I did not. Fortuitous for sure, but I didn't do it. Dalton sagged a little on the desk he'd been standing next to when Vance spoke to him through their link. *There are other players in on this thing, Dalton. You might want to gird up your loins and become better armed. All of us should.*

Do you know who did this? Vance said he had an idea but couldn't share just yet. *And this person, the one that murdered these men, you think he's after the dragon as well? That he's got it in his head to kill off the women when they get them?*

Yes. It was a simple answer, but terrifying as well. *This man, and lets just call him Smith, he's playing a different game than the others. He wants all the pieces, and will not stop until he gets*

163

them.

You know this for a certainty? Vance said he did. *And what does he plan to do with them? I mean, if he kills us all off, the dragon can't come out anyway.*

He hopes to sell them to someone who has his eye on the future. Not ours, but one that our children's children will inherit. Dalton asked him how that was going to be possible if they killed the women. *I don't think he's thought it through all the way to the end conclusion. But his plan, while not really workable, will make him a very wealthy man, as well as all of us dead.*

Dalton instructed the men with him to look for anything that might be a clue. Vance told him that there would be nothing, the man was that good. Dalton told him he had to do something. It was that or feel like he'd failed somehow. Vance assured him that he had not.

Do you know where any more of the pieces of jewelry are? Or perhaps if anyone else has them? I'd really hate to think of some poor woman out there trying on something that she liked, and being killed before she has a chance to figure out she needs to come to us. He said that he was keeping an eye out for them. *Vance, what is it you do? I mean…what are you?*

Your brother. Dalton wasn't satisfied with that answer, and he was sure that his brother knew it. *All right, but you're going to wish you'd just left it at I'm your brother. I'm with the Special Forces. And by that I mean I do what the government tells me and how they tell me. I kill what needs to be killed. Kidnap who needs to be questioned. Sometimes there is very little difference, but I do it. I'm a ghost, a shadow that lurks in corners and comes out on the other side with a knife or gun. I'm not a good person. And I haven't been for a very long time.*

Dalton didn't believe that any more than he did he was going to find a clue in this house. Vance might do things that were scary, but he was a good man. A great man he thought. But he could hear the fatigue in his voice, see it on his body when he was around them all.

Are you all right, Vance? I mean, you're okay, aren't you? He asked him what he meant. *You sound.... Well, I've been a cop for a very long time, and I can see that you're beginning to show signs of being burnt out. Sometimes, even when you're home, you're not there. How much longer can you do this?*

Someone has to. Dalton told him that wasn't an answer. *I don't know. You and the others, you can have your pretty lives. I don't think.... Hell, Dalton, I know that any woman out there for me is going to have to be saintly. Stronger than even Emma is to be with me. As I said, I'm not a good person.*

I think you're a wonderful person. When Vance said nothing, Dalton decided it was time to change the subject for now. But he would talk to Vance, maybe convince him that he was better than he thought. *We know that someone shot Wilburn first. Then Richard when he came in second. We know this thanks to the security cameras on the front of the house. But what we don't know and can't find is who the shooter is.*

He's not going to be on the cameras, and even if he was, it's doubtful that you'd be able to make him out. Dalton asked if he was human. *Yes. He is. Most of the men working for him are as well.*

Do you know if he killed them over the jewelry? Vance said that he had. *I see. So we have someone in this town that will kill whoever gets in his way.*

Pretty much. But he doesn't live in the area. He only came here...if this is the man I think it is, he only came here to kill these two. Which I have to admit, they had served their purpose anyway. Dalton didn't want to think what that meant. *The bugs that were planted in your office, as well as one in Jorden's, they're from*

Richard. You're going to be able to figure that out now that you have his body. Wilburn is the one that put the second one in Jorden's office, and in the antique shop as well. I'll have them removed now that there is no one listening in on them.

This other player, do you think he'll set up more of the same? Vance said he wasn't sure, but he'd let him know when he did. *I'd like that. Thank you.*

I have to go away for a bit. Shouldn't be any longer than about a month. Dalton started to ask him what was going on, but Vance cut that thought off. *Don't ask me. As much as I'd like to tell you it's fine, it's not, and I don't want to have to explain what I'm doing to you. Leave it alone.*

Will you be safe, at least? Vance told him he was forever safe. But for some reason, Dalton didn't believe him.

I'll keep in contact with you should I hear any more about this other man. All right?

Yes. But I wish you'd let me know more. Vance told him he didn't want to know. *Perhaps. But at least I'd know if I need to call in the others if I don't hear from you.*

If you don't hear from me, I'm dead. And there would be nothing that any of you could do but get yourself dead as well. Stay safe.

Dalton felt the loss of connection immediately and profoundly. As he stood in the middle of his crime scene, all Dalton wanted to do was hunt Vance down and hug him. He wasn't sure how he'd take that, but that was all he wanted to do. When someone said his name, it took him a few seconds to think what he was doing. Dalton took the file that he was handed.

"Found this in the bottom of the drawer. Well, under the drawer. You told us to look for something out of the ordinary, and I saw this program once where the bad guys would hide things in plain sight under their desk drawers." Dalton wanted to ask the rookie if he did all his police work from drama shows, but decided that he had enough truth today and only opened the file. "I believe it's about your family."

There were pictures of his entire family, including Emma and Jasmine. Two blurry pictures of their mom, as well as a couple dozen of Gavin. On the back of each one was some notes, patterns that whoever wrote it had picked up. Dalton was reading how he stopped by the bakery every Wednesday morning and flirted for two minutes with the woman behind the counter, then got his tea and moved on. Kenton arrived at his office at eight-thirty and sat in his office for ten minutes just playing a game on his computer.

Dalton looked at his watch and picked up his phone. He needed the contact that a phone call could give him, for some reason. When Kenton answered his phone with some irritation, Dalton asked him if he was losing.

"Losing what?" Dalton looked at the note and told him the name of the game. "Sort of. How did you know I was...? Is my office bugged?"

"No. But you've been studied. In four minutes you're going to turn off your game, reboot your computer, and put on your jacket for the day. Once you have opened your doors, your day begins." Kenton sounded worried when he asked him who had told him that. "I'm standing in the middle of Glass's office with two dead bodies. My officers, one of them, found this file on all of us. Even Mom."

"They're watching us?" Dalton said they had been. "I see. And this means that we can more than likely expect more of the same until all of us are with our mates."

"I would assume so. Not only that, but I think it'll get worse as it goes on. The last person to join us, she'll be.... I don't even know what to think she'll have to endure to become one of our mates." Dalton didn't want to think about finding a mate. It wasn't that he didn't want one, but he was sort of thinking he'd like to find her on his own. Not because some dragon had deemed her to be his. "Kenton, we need to have a family meeting. Soon."

"I agree. I just heard from Vance. He's going to be on some kind of sabbatical for a few weeks. I think he needs to rest up some too." Dalton said nothing, knowing that that his brother had lied to Kenton for some reason. "How about we all meet here tonight? I think that Gavin and Mom are working on their thing at my house with Emma, and I think that Jorden leaves in a few weeks too, so he's trying to get ready for his show."

"I'll be there. Can I bring anything? Empty container for left overs? Maybe a cooler or two for desserts to take home?" They both laughed, and he looked at his men when he realized he'd been on the phone for too long. "I have to go. If things get cleared up here sooner, I'll give you a call and we can get together for a quick meeting before."

By the time he was ready to call it a day they'd found more files on other women, and he forwarded them on to Vance. He figured he'd have the best chance of finding them and keeping them safe. There was also a long list of people who owed money to Wilburn, as well as a diary of sorts about Richard. Wilburn hadn't cared for his brother much, it seemed. Dalton also found a thumb drive, which he plugged into his computer at his home instead of at work. He had no idea why, but he thought it might be something no one at work needed to hear about.

"Hello. I'm not sure which officer found this, but I have to say that I'm surprised that you took the time to play this." There was no view of the man talking, but the camera focused on a dead Wilburn. "Before we get going much further, I should like for you to go and find Kenton McCade — he's a physician of some high standards — or even one of the others. They talk to one another, so whoever you find is good. I should like for you to pause here for you to find them."

Dalton thought about going to get his brothers, but decided that there might be something on there to give him some idea as to who this person was. He had no doubt that he'd been the murderer, but there might have been more. Some of which he might not want his family to see or hear.

"Well, good. Welcome. I'm not going to bore you with my name. Suffice it to say, I'm not one of your friends. In fact, it would be easy to say that I'm your worst enemy. That being said, I want you to know that I'm going to get all the pieces of the *demi parvure* that you search for. And yes, that would include the two that you already have. And when I do get them, and there is no doubt that I will, I will sell them to the highest bidder and be richer than I am at present."

Dalton started making notes. Not at what the man was saying, but any key words he could pick out, like how he pronounced certain words such as *richer* and *am*. He'd already figured out that the man was intelligent, well-educated, and wealthy. He would also bet that he worked alone and had no second man, no one to betray him or to know anything about him other than what he needed him to. Dalton thought this man was going to be very dangerous.

"I have my eye on two more of the pieces. So many believe there are only five, but I know there are six. The necklace, being too heavy for a woman, had been broken down and made into two of the most beautiful torques ever seen. Then when that too became too cumbersome, they were made into a single one. The dragons are chasing one another around the arm. I also know that they each have a gem in their mouth. One a

169

blue diamond, the other a rare blue opal." Dalton leaned back in his seat as the man continued. "Yes, I know a great deal about each piece. I would go so far as to say that someone I am related to might have had a hand in their design.

"But I digress. The woman that has the earrings, explain to her that her son will live a great deal longer if she were just to let me kill her. I know, I know, you're thinking me cold. Well, you'd be correct. But I'm also willing to kill a woman to get just what I want. The other woman, she too will die at my scalpel." Dalton paused in his writing again to replay that last line. *She too will die at my scalpel.*

Not knife. Scalpel. Dalton continued the recording on the drive until the end. The man talked about his plans, how much money he was going to ask for the pieces, then he went on to say how he wouldn't kill the men, not the McCades, unless he had to.

"What do I care if there is another generation of your family? So long as the other person, my buyer, has no idea that he's bought something that will never come to fruition." Dalton thought the man had already planned to kill them all anyway. He'd think it more fun to know that someone was shit out of luck about the dragon coming to life. "One more thing I should tell you about. The woman who will bring you the next piece, the hair combs? She's sadly dead."

Dalton pulled the drive out and sat there for several minutes. He was glad now that he'd found it and not anyone else. Nor had he added it to the inventory that they'd logged from the house. This was something that no one but his family needed to know about. He looked at the drive again, wondering about the man who had recorded it.

There had been nothing to show his face. No hands nor any part of the man had been shown at all. He was meticulous in his words. The camera or whatever device he'd used hadn't been found at the scene. So far there had been no prints found, other than those of the two men and the housekeeper who had found them. Nothing, so far as he could see, was missing. Who was this man?

Vance. He had to get this to him and let him look it over. Grabbing up his jacket and gun, Dalton moved out of his office, reaching for his brother at the same time.

I'm at the airport now. Not the commercial one, but on the base. I'll have them allow you in. Dalton thought about that for all of a second until Vance laughed. *No one will shoot you so long as you cooperate with them. Which means, if you're armed, you hand it over nicely.*

Sure. And will I get it back? Vance said if he was a good boy. *I don't care for you at the moment.*

Driving to the base, Dalton thought of something else. He needed to talk to Kenton or Jorden. Perhaps the dragon knew if someone had been killed as yet. Making a mental note of all the things he needed to do, Dalton thought that whoever this guy was, he had fucked with the wrong family.

CHAPTER 12

Grady tried his best not to get upset. But the man he'd been working with for over an hour wasn't listening to him. Nor would he stop clicking the fucking mouse when whatever he wanted done wasn't moving fast enough. Then when the computer seized up for the fourth time in an hour, the man looked at him.

"You're not doing a very good job at making this work correctly. I have told you several times that it's running slowly, and you said that it wasn't that. Well? What the hell is it if it's not the computer?" It was on the tip of Grady's tongue to say it was all on him, but he only took the mouse from the man and put it on the table behind him. "And how do you suppose I make this thing work? By using my mind?"

"No. What I want is for you to be patient, as I have said to you several times now. You cannot keep opening the same page over and over and not expect it to clog up your computer. As it is right now, you have...." Grady counted the open tabs, and before he was finished, six more opened. "You have twenty-nine of the same page open. The same graphics are running on each of them, as well as the chat person is there. All twenty-nine of them waiting to help you with your order."

"You must have done that. I only wanted the one page open. And if you say differently, I'm going to call your boss. You're a rude man, has anyone told you that before?" Grady said nothing but did stand up. Enough was enough, he thought. "And where do you think you're going? I have paid for you to come here and fix my computer. I will not be happy if you leave me here stranded."

"Mr. Williams, I have done all that I can. I have shown you several times what you need to do. If you just close out all but one of those programs, you'll see that things work better." He noticed that while he'd been talking to the man, four more pages had popped up. "In a moment your computer is going to seize up again, and then you'll need to reboot. I'm sorry I can't help you, but you have a nice day."

He was out the door and on the sidewalk before he let out the breath he'd been holding. Mr. Williams was lonely; he knew that was his only reason for calling the company that Grady worked for. And the old man would request him, even waiting for a day or two until he could work him in. As he got into his truck, his cell phone was ringing and he saw it was work.

"Mr. Williams just called in. He's not happy with you. He said that he might not request you any more if you keep that up." Grady told him good. "I need for you to go over to the university and see what is up with their server. I'd go, but I have this meeting at home to attend."

Doug Norton always had something to attend or something that needed his attention. The man spent less time at work than the cleaning crew did that came in once a week. And when Grady had asked him for a raise, something to show that all his hard work was paying off, he'd told him that things were tight and that he was barely making it any more.

So being Grady, he'd looked into the man's finances as well as the business. The company was doing poorly, but he thought it was because Doug was taking all the profits. Grady had found that not only did he have a nice speed boat with all the trimmings, but he had three cars in his name, a house here and one in England where his wife was from, and all his children went to private schools. No, the business wasn't failing, it was being robbed.

"I need to ask you for a raise." He heard Doug groan, something he did a lot lately. "I've been working for you for the last six years, and I'd like to have a cost of living raise. I deserve it."

"Yes, you do. All the people who work for me do. But I can't swing it. Not now. I have things coming up…taxes to pay. You have no idea what it's like to have a business of your own and what it costs to run it." The idea that he'd been tossing around in his head surfaced while Doug went on about this and that. "You understand, don't you, buddy? I just can't swing it, not now anyway."

"Then I'm sorry, but I have to quit. I have two weeks of pay coming for vacation, and you can keep that instead of me giving you two weeks' notice." Doug started sputtering then and Grady felt great, like something heavy had been lifted from his chest. "I'll come in now and turn in my beeper and jacket. Since I paid for my shirts and tools, those are mine to keep. If you're not there, please instruct Dana to give me —"

"Hold on there. You can't leave me. You're my best worker." Grady didn't tell him that he was his only worker, as the others were as lazy as their boss and all related to him. He didn't think a single one of them knew a hard drive from

175

a thumb drive. "I tell you what, Grady, I'll swing some extra cash your way. I can manage about twenty-five more a week, but that's about it. I'm cutting it close every month now."

"Then this should help you out. I'm done, Doug. I can't work for a man who has no respect for what I can give to the job." Doug was talking thirty then thirty-five more a week when Grady cut him off. "I'm at the offices now. I'll just turn my things in and be on my way."

"You can't do that to me. Damn it, Grady, what the hell is up your ass? You're just overworked, I think. You take a couple of days off—I'll even pay you for them—and you think this over. Then when you have, I'll sit down with you and we can talk about a raise. All right?"

Grady smiled at Dana as he closed his phone. "I'm done." She asked him if he'd hit the university. "No, I mean I'm done with this job. I'm turning in the beeper and name badge. If you don't mind, I'd like a receipt for them."

"You're quitting? Now?" He said that he had quit, he'd told Doug. "But you can't quit. Who will do these jobs? Christ, the shit is about to hit the fan, Grady, and you're fucking it up."

"I don't care. A receipt please. Or I can call my brother, Dalton, in to witness that I gave my things to you." She jerked the things out of his hand and wrote out a receipt. When he looked at what she'd written, he laughed. "Fucktard Grady McCade turned in one beeper and one name badge that belongs to the company."

Before she made a copy of it for her records, he wrote on the bottom the date, time, and that he was giving his two weeks of vacation for his notice. Then he signed that as well. The phone was ringing while he stood there, and she said she wasn't answering it. They both knew it was Doug.

Going out to his truck again, he left the property before he had to pull over and turn off his engine. He'd just quit his job. It sucked, paid badly, but it was his job. An income. Not that he needed to work, but he didn't touch his savings account at all. And he wouldn't now, not if he could help it. He realized he was in front of the business district and made his way there.

Pulling his phone out of his pocket, he looked at the number of missed calls. Doug had called him a total of fourteen times and had left three messages since he'd talked to him. Grady was glad now that he'd muted his phone when he'd gone to Mr. Williams's house earlier. Tossing the phone into the truck, he made his way to Winder Avenue where he owned one of the many buildings.

Doug just called here. Congratulations. He grinned at Jorden's comment. *You should have quit long ago.*

I know that now. Christ, I feel both terrified and elated at the same time. I'm here looking over buildings now. I'm going to run Doug and his shitty business out of town. Jorden laughed. *But seriously, what did he say to you? Did he try and tell you what a fool I am?*

He didn't actually talk to me, but Jasmine. And so you know, I don't think he'll call here again. Grady asked what she'd told him. *Well, if he ever gets his balls out of the mental vise that she put him in, I'm pretty sure he'll figure out that none of us are going to be talking you into going back to work for him. I think she might have told him of a couple of places that he could shove his need for you to come and talk to him that I wasn't aware that a human might have. She also 'warned' him not to call any of the rest of us. If he does, I'm thinking that I'll need to have a really good show so I can bail Jasmine out of jail.*

I'll help you. He entered the building and looked around. *I'm going to open my new business in the district. Help Emma and*

Jasmine with their project. I have enough capital, so I should be able to sell computers, not just fix them.

Good. If you need any funding, Emma and Jasmine have set up this Loan to Work place that you can apply for grants as well as government low interest loans to get help. He said he'd think on it. *Well, I'm in the middle of painting this...I have a project that I'm working on here, so I have to get going.*

After closing the connection, Grady looked at what he was going to have to do to get up and running. The place had been a shoe store once, and then later it had been a small engine repair place as well. He noticed that a lot of the shelving as well as a counter had been left behind. And he found an office that he loved.

Your lordship, she is coming. Grady stood perfectly still when the voice spoke to him. He knew it was in his mind, but it made him no less terrified. *She has...the piece that she has, I cannot tell what it is. She will not tell me either.*

Stubborn, is she? Caelin said that she was most stubborn. *And since I can suddenly hear you, I'm assuming that she's my mate. Coming here to be with me.*

I didn't know it until you answered me. I tried the others first... Vance was my first pick, and I thought that he was perhaps ignoring me. But then I tried Dalton and Lewis, with the same results. Grady wasn't sure how he felt about being his last pick, but said nothing. *She has the piece in her possession, but she will not put it on. Should she do that, I would be able to speak to the both of you at the same time. As I have said, she is very stubborn.*

I thought that they had to wear whatever piece was given to them in order for this to work. Caelin said he'd thought that as well. *So, she's different then. I wonder why?*

I don't know her name. Nor if she is alone in her journey here. Grady asked him if she was coming here. *Yes, she wishes to get this finished, she said, so that I will leave her alone. I think she believes she only has to hand it over to the family and that will be the end of things. And as she will not let me into her mind by wearing the piece, then I can only tell her what I know and where to go.*

Grady was beginning to like this woman a great deal. She was thwarting things for the dragon, and if she could do that, perhaps she would be able to survive the people trying to find her. He asked Caelin if anyone was trying to harm her.

I know not, my lord. I only know that she has woken the piece up, but nothing more. And as you know, only the female can do that. She has it still, but that is all I know. Grady laughed again. *It is most infuriating to have her not answer my questions, sir. She should know that I am most persistent and let me help her when I can.*

I think she's going to be your greatest pain in the ass, and I for one am glad for it. You need to have your life shaken up once in a while. Caelin asked him if he was happy that he'd had his shaken. *Yes. I think I am. I'm afraid, but I'm excited too. I can make this work for me.*

If anyone can make this work, it shall be you, my lord. Grady started to ask why he was calling him that and decided it was fine. So long as no one else did it. As he sat there, thinking about what he was going to do, he thought of the woman.

Grady would have to make changes in his life. First and foremost, the house he'd been given. While he did stay there, saying that he lived there would have been grossly overstated. It was a place that he slept in a couple of times a week. He wanted to get it ready for her, perhaps do some of the things around the house that he'd been thinking about. It was time, Grady thought, to become a man of worth.

~~~

He moved along the buildings, careful where he stepped.

179

A man in his position was not one to have scuffed shoes nor a smudged suit. He had a great many things to do after this, and he wasn't going to be happy with this woman if she did not do as he wished. He had no idea why they had to be so stupid when it was obvious they were caught by a man such as himself.

The door in front of him opened suddenly and he had to step back from the vile odor coming from the man there. It was tempting to pull out his weapon and end his miserable life, but there wasn't enough time today. The man did not know how lucky he was.

When he spotted her again, he moved in that direction. She was sly, he'd give her that. Going in and out of the market like she was, it was difficult to keep tabs on her. But today had to be the day; he had information on another piece of the demi set.

Standing in the spot where he'd seen her again, he had to turn in a full circle to get his bearings. Twice now she had eluded him, and he was getting upset with the cat and mouse games she was playing. When he saw her again, he picked up his pace to end this.

Fredrick prided himself on a great many things. He wasn't perfect, but few knew that. Taking a right instead of a left, he knew, would cut her off and put him in the position to kill her and take her piece. As soon as he turned into the empty alley, he realized his mistake. She had taken another avenue.

The buyer he had lined up was one that he'd been talking to for months now. As soon as he was able to show him the goods — what a horrid name for something so expensive — he was going to be getting a sizable deposit from him. Fredrick didn't need the money, but he knew that he could always have more. And that was something he wanted. If he couldn't have it all, he wanted more.

The earpiece buzzing told him he had an incoming call. Answering it with a stern warning to the caller, he waited for someone to speak. He should have looked at his phone to see who it was, but he was busy and the caller should have known that.

"Having any luck?" He had no idea who the voice belonged to so said nothing. "I'm thinking that you're not. Could be because you're stupid, but I don't think that's it. Perhaps it's just that you have no idea what you're up against."

"Who is this?" The person laughed, a sound that was eerily scary as well as confident. "I asked you a question and I demand that you answer me."

"Well, who died and left you king of shit? Oh wait. When people piss you off they don't die, they are murdered. By you. When I get you, and I will, I'm going to extract payment for each of them from your body." The vision of what the man was saying popped into his head.

Fredrick was laying on a table, his body tied there, naked as the day he'd been born. The man, hooded and dark, stood over him with a knife, brilliantly lit in the moonlight. His body was covered in blood, his own blood, and there were cuts and bruises all over him. When the knife blade came down again, Fredrick could—

"Do you see it, Fredrick? Or should I call you by your given name? Bobby Ware. Do you think the children you went to school with still call you Bobby Pin behind your back? A boy as small as you was called a great many names, weren't you, Bobby?" Fredrick leaned heavily against the wall behind him, thoughts of the girl and her jewelry gone. The man knew a lot, too much.

"Where are you? Who have you been talking to? I demand

that you tell me where you got this information." The man laughed again, and this time Fredrick could almost see him throwing back his head in his humor. "Who are you?"

"Your worst nightmare, as a matter of fact. A man that is going to ruin you first, then kill you. Perhaps with my bare hands." The same vision came to him. Only this time the man was strangling him, his large hands wrapped tightly around his throat. "I shall enjoy making you beg me with your eyes. Telling me with your last breath that you need to live. Yes, I think I shall enjoy this a great deal."

He felt his bladder loosen and his balls tighten painfully. Fredrick did not like pain, not even to bump his hand against something. But this man was talking to him as if he knew for a fact that he was going to kill him, even knowing how it would be done. When he laughed again, Fredrick told him he was hanging up.

"Before you do, I would like to give you one last chance. Stay away from the girl. All of them, as a matter of fact." Fredrick asked him why he'd do that. "Because they're mine. The jewels, the women, even the men, they're mine. I'm going to rule them all, and the dragon will bring me wealth that no one can imagine, not even you."

"I've a great deal invested in this. Why do you think I'll just walk away from it all? I mean, riches beyond compare? The sale that I have lined up alone is more than most people would see in several lifetimes." He saw the girl then; she stood just across from where he stood, her body turned so that he could see that she was talking on the phone. He'd been chasing her for weeks now, and would end this once and for all. "I'm not going to quit, just so you know. And if you know what's good for you, you'll stop what you're doing and know that you've given it your best shot."

He was nearly to her when a man with a dark hoodie came up behind her. Before he could warn her, if that was even in his plan, the man pulled her head back and slit her throat. Then he turned her in his direction so that he could see that she was bleeding out. Fredrick asked him what he was doing?

"Why, I'm collecting on what is mine. And so you know, the others will not die as quickly or as quietly." He dropped her body then and stepped over her when a crowd began to gather. "They'll find your prints on the knife, Fredrick. If I were you, I'd run."

The sirens sounded close by, too soon after the murder for them to have been alerted. Fredrick knew that they'd been called prior to it, and had an inkling that he had been named as a suspect. As he backed from the crime scene and the body laying inert on the ground, he tried to think what he could do now. The man had said that his prints were on the weapon. That they would be after him.

Going to his car, he had his driver take him home. It was the only place he felt safe right now. As he gathered notes, things to run with, he tried to remain calm, think so that he'd leave no traces of where he was going behind. Fredrick wasn't going to be caught. Not in this lifetime.

Things were put in order; his car, the one he was going to drive, was packed up, money at the ready. As soon as he got word that the police were coming to him, he would be gone, nowhere to be found. An hour after he was home, he began to worry less. Then an hour turned into two, then four. Fredrick thought that the man had fooled him.

And he'd made a fool of him. Fredrick was not one to trifle with, he thought, and this man, whoever he was, he'd pay for this. And in the worst way possible. As he began to relax, his body worn out from all the unnecessary stress, he decided that he needed to figure out if the woman had indeed been killed. For all he knew that, too, could have been a ruse.

His butler came to get him just as it was time for dinner. As he entered his dining room, he looked around. He wanted nothing out of place, nothing to mar the beauty of his home. Just as he was seated, his first course set before him, he heard the front bell. Thinking nothing of it, he told Marco to tell the intruder to go away. Business was not conducted after five.

Taking a sip of his soup, careful not to look greedy, he found himself on the floor with a boot at his throat. Before he could ask what the meaning of this was, he looked up at the hooded man. When he pulled out a gun and pointed it at him, Fredrick had a single thought before the man fired. Where was the jewelry?

Now Available in the McCade Dragon Series

Before You Go...

HELP AN AUTHOR

write a review

THANK YOU!

Share your voice and help guide other readers to these wonderful books. Even if it's only a line or two your reviews help readers discover the author's books so they can continue creating stories that you'll love. Login to your favorite retailer and leave a review. Thank you.

AWARD WINNING, BESTSELLING AUTHOR

Kathi Barton, author of the bestselling series Force of Nature, lives in Nashport, Ohio with her husband Paul. In addition to writing full time Kathi likes to spend time with her eight grandkids, three children and three children-in-laws. She writes to relax and have fun.

Her muse, a cross between Jimmy Stewart and Hugh Jackman brings them to life for her readers in a way that has them coming back time and again for more. Her favorite genre is paranormal romance with a great deal of spice. You can visit Kathi online and drop her an email if you'd like. She loves hearing from her fans. aaronskiss@gmail.com.

Follow Kathi on her blog: http://kathisbartonauthor.blogspot.com/

www.ingramcontent.com/pod-product-compliance
Lightning Source LLC
Chambersburg PA
CBHW032139170626
46808CB00006B/2302